SUNG IN
BLOOD

SUNG IN
BLOOD

GLEN COOK

NIGHT SHADE BOOKS
NEW YORK

Night Shade books may be purchased in bulk at special
discounts for sales promotion, corporate gifts, fund-
raising, or educational purposes. Special editions can
also be created to specifications. For details, contact the
Special Sales Department, Night Shade Books, 307
West 36th Street, 11th Floor, New York, NY 10018 or
info@skyhorsepublishing.com.

Night Shade Books™ is a trademark of Skyhorse Publishing,
Inc. ®, a Delaware corporation.

Visit our website at www.nightshadebooks.com.

10 9 8 7 6 5 4 3 2 1

Library of Congress Cataloging-in-Publication Data is
available on file.

ISBN: 978-1-59780-505-6

Printed in the United States of America

I

Death stalked the night. It haunted the shadowed alleys of Shasesserre.

Those it passed near hurried away, driven by the knives of fear.

Death wore the guise of a squat, gnarly man in a vile yellow mask, the mask of a *shantor*, a carrier of the weeping sickness.

Death was a liar, a wearer of false faces.

The gnarly man zigzagged the darkest ways, hurrying toward the City's heart—the Plaza of Jehrke Victorious. Across his back he carried a rag-wrapped bundle. He reached the edge of the great square. Beyond, the Rock and its crown, Citadel Nibroc, reared their humped and spiky silhouettes against the stars.

It was a rare and cloud-clear night there at the crossroads 'twixt land and sea.

Between plaza's edge and Citadel stood a five-hundred-foot temporary needle of timbers, kept upright by scores of guylines. The masked man paused to see if he was observed, then ran to its foot. He swarmed upward with the tireless energy of a machine. When he reached the crowning platform, from which rope divers would plunge during tomorrow's celebrations, he was barely panting.

The gnarly man shed his burden. For a moment he stared at the nearest spire of the Citadel, then began ripping rags off his bundle. Starlight glinted off steel and polished wood. He began assembling some mysterious engine.

A moist breeze off the Golden Crescent lifted his yellow mask. It betrayed an evil, gap-toothed murderer's grin.

Jehrke entered his laboratory almost furtively. His lamp illuminated a face gaunt with worry, with fear.

The Protector afraid? Impossible. For three centuries his wizardry had nurtured and shielded Shasesserre in a world that hungered to rape its wealth and plunder its power. He had brushed aside a thousand perils. He had survived a thousand threats. His might and skill were legend.

"It's *him*! But how does he come, that I do not smell him in every shadow?" His web of sorcery lay everywhere upon the City. No magician great or feeble, white or dark, could evade his notice. "The breath of him stinks. And what better time to strike?"

Jehrke moved about, lighting lamps. They revealed a laboratory that would have amazed his most advanced colleagues. "Through what dark crack does he design to thrust his wickedness?"

Shasesserre remained Queen of the Orient, Crossroad of the World, because for three centuries no shadow had leaked past Jehrke's vigilance. There was a saying: "Good or bad, Kings and Queens come and go. Jehrke is forever."

It was a time of a good King, and the Protector, and all at the heart of the world prospered.

But wolves howled beyond the border, dark and jealous. Their master kept them whipped to a frenzy.

Jehrke looked out the window on the night, on the constellation that was the city that never sleeps. The hairs on his neck bristled. A chill made him shudder.

He turned gaunt face and hollow eyes toward a map of Shasesserre's domains. "Can there be a rent in the fabric of the web? Has he found some way to steal close unremarked?" He scowled at the chart. It told him nothing he had not known for centuries.

Suddenly, he whirled to face the window. He knew he felt death's cold breath and clammy touch.

Cursing, the gnarly man hammered a wooden frame member with his fist. It snapped into place. He glanced at the newly lighted window. The man passed the light.

The gnarly fellow cursed again and furiously pumped a crank on the side of his engine. Wood creaked. Steel scraped, a large coil spring wound tighter and tighter.

"He must die. The Master has condemned him. He must die tonight."

Finished cranking, he gazed through a metal tube attached to his device. He adjusted its position. Satisfied, he tripped a wooden lever. The engine creaked as the coil spring drove gears and pulleys and hauled back the string of the massive crossbow that was the machine's heartpiece.

A short arrow, or long quarrel, dropped from a hopper into the channel of the crossbow.

Three hundred yards away the doomed man faced a map, back to the window, centered within its rectangle. The gnarly man tripped another lever and dove for the ladder down. Behind him the death engine thunked and began to rewind.

A terrible cry ripped the fabric of the night. It shook the foundations of the Rock. A bleak and horrible wind bowled through the Plaza of Jehrke Victorious. The gnarly assassin clung to the ladder four hundred eighty feet above cobblestones and shrieked entreaties to heathen gods.

The wind departed as suddenly as it came. The killer resumed his scramble toward the ground.

Above, the death machine creaked and thunked methodically.

The first bolt shattered the window and hit Jehrke an inch above the heart. It flung him back against the map. Nine of its eighteen inches buried themselves in the wall.

Direct physical assault! Never had he considered the chance of an attack so unsubtle.

Agony tore his flesh. Almost, his control slipped as he screamed a death-curse that sent his web into insane paroxysms. He gestured with his left hand. Pale fire crawled about the laboratory. He gestured with his right. Shadows flew out into the storm, toward the diving tower, only possible point for launching the attack.

The next bolt arrived. The Protector jerked, then

sagged. Soon another missile thumped home. Then another; and another, in regular, deadly rhythm.

II

There were five people in the room with the pin-cushioned Protector. None were ordinary, but the eye tended to a grim-faced fellow in imperial Ride-Master of Cavalry uniform. He was tall, well-muscled, with arcticly cold blue eyes. He paced like a captive panther, restless grace in a cage. He was the last to arrive.

"We tried to find you as soon as Chaz told us, Rider," said a moonfaced imp of a fellow. He *was* an imp. He tried hard to look human, but yellow fangs lapped his fat lower lips and his eyes were all oily ruby pupil. Puffs of sulphurous smoke occasionally escaped his wide nostrils. "But you was on patrol, Captain."

The imp's name was Su-Cha. He was the Ride-Master's familiar, kept in this world as one of his several associates.

The other three present were human men, but odd in their ways.

Chaz was a giant barbarian from the far north. In most ways he was faithful to stereotype. He enjoyed busting things up. Near Chaz stood a nut-brown, rail-thin, beetle-faced easterner whose hobby was crafting odd machines. His name was Omar and a lot more, but his friends called him Spud. The third man looked like a derelict, with wild white hair and beard, and clothing little better than rags. He had to be reminded to change. He used the name Greystone. He spent his attention on studying and thinking, not his appearance.

"Where's Preacher? Where's Soup?" the man with the frosty eyes asked, about members of the group not present.

"Looking for you," said Su-Cha. "Unless they got distracted by some floozy."

Rider—for so he was called by his friends—faced the corpse of the man who had been his father, for the first time squarely. "He knew it would come. But he didn't expect it this soon, nor this way."

"Three hundred years," Chaz intoned. "Hard to believe, Rider. Even that way he looks too young."

The younger Jehrke's eyes grew colder. "The torch has been passed, ready or not."

"We're ready, Rider," Su-Cha said. "Let's get at it."

Rider ignored the imp. "Chaz. You're sure nobody has gotten in here? That only we and the assassins know?"

"I was with him. He just wanted to check something, he said. I waited outside. I started to wonder how come he was taking so long. Then he yelled. When I broke in he was like that."

Rider went to the window, glared at the tower in the Plaza. Though festivities were not to start for hours, spectators had begun to assemble. "They came from the diving platform. You went to find Su-Cha. How long were you gone?"

"Two minutes."

"Then there was no time for an intruder to destroy any message my father left."

"Message? We would've found one if—"

Rider raised a hand. He cocked his head. "You hear anything?" he asked Su-Cha, indicating the door.

The imp shook his head but glided that way. He

was accustomed to Rider's finely tuned senses. The dead wizard had raised his son to stretch every human capacity. At the door the imp vaporized. He reassumed corporeality moments later. "Nobody. But there may have been someone. The sand you scattered was disturbed." Among other attributes Su-Cha had a perfect memory for the most minuscule details.

Rider merely nodded. He assembled various items from the laboratory, performed a slight magic. Then he dusted a handful of orange powder upon a blank piece of wall. Chaz gasped. "Parts of words."

"My father's final message. I've long suspected it was there, awaiting his death to activate it." He stepped up to the wall, passed a palm over the message. The powder fluoresced.

Son. Your hour is come. I have prepared you as well as I could. Protect Shasesserre from the wolves without and worms within. Always there will be enemies of tranquility and prosperity. You will be occupied continuously. Their wickedness knows no proportion. In the bathhouse on the Saverne side, in the place I once showed you, you will find the names of those who must be watched.

"He updated that list frequently," Rider said. "I didn't know he kept it there, though."

Do not waste time mourning me. Shasesserre's enemies will not. They will be moving before you read this.

Your father

The elder Jehrke had had difficulty expressing affection even in writing.

"There it is." Rider brushed a palm over the wall again. The message vanished. He went to the window. "Chaz. You said there was a howl outside?"

"Yes."

Rider stared at the Plaza. "How long will his name remain, now? He was not the sort to eradicate his enemies. There must be a dozen cabals awaiting this chance. One is moving already. We'll have to act fast if we're to grab the reins before word gets out."

Some of his companions nodded. Chaz grunted. It was something they had discussed often. Though no traditional dictator, Jehrke had maintained himself as Protector by the terror he instilled in those who would plunder Shasesserre. With the Protector gone, any number of strongmen would attempt to prevent his ideals being perpetuated. Among them could be counted nobles, high officials, churchmen, rich men of trade, even gangsters. Not to mention the Queen City's foreign enemies.

"Chaos," Rider said. "We look that dragon right in the mouth."

"Surely there will be popular support for the son to continue the work of the father."

"There will be. But ordinary people do not wield the power. The men who would see my father's ideals put aside care not about the popular voice. The voices they hear are power and greed."

The imp, Su-Cha, murmured, "Then there are those who hearken overmuch to the siren call of revenge."

Rider acted as though he had not heard. He said, "We'd better examine that tower. The assassin might have left a clue."

The group piled out of the room. None of the others noticed that Rider delayed a few seconds before joining them.

III

Preacher and Soup were headed for the Rock. "Somebody found him by now," Soup said.

"Verily." Preacher was so called because of his dress, manner of speech, and his incessant efforts to convert his comrades to a baffling dogma endemic to his native Frista. It was doubted even he took himself seriously. He yielded to temptation too easily.

The two rounded a corner and found themselves face to face with a short, gnarly man who looked remarkably like a bull gorilla. The gnarly man's eyes bugged. He gaped. He whirled and ran.

"The evil flee where no man pursueth," Preacher intoned.

"You said a mouthful, brother. Want to bet that geek had something to do with croaking Rider's old man?"

"Gambling is a snare of the devil," Preacher replied. "No bet. Let's get him."

"I got a better idea. Let's see where he goes. He's heading up Floral. Looked like a foreigner. Maybe he don't know you can cut through Bleek Alley."

"I'll take the alley. You run him."

"Lazy." Preacher had that reputation.

"He's gaining."

That gnarly man could move for having such short legs.

"The wings of fear carrieth the wicked."

"Stuff it, Preach. Cut out and head him off."

Preacher ducked into Bleek Alley, black clothing flying around him. It was a dark, twisting way little more than the span of his arms wide, filled with trash and shadows.

One clot of shadow coughed up a swarm of gnarly men. "Ambush!" Preacher gasped. Footsteps hammered behind him. There was no exit.

Preacher never backed down from a fight. And he was five times tougher than he talked, ten times tougher than he looked. He let rip one great bloody shriek and hurled himself forward.

His attack astonished them. Long thin arms tipped by fists as hard as rocks hammered them. The gnarly men grunted as the blows fell, got tangled as they tried to reorganize. Preacher produced a sand-filled leather sap and started thumping heads. Two gnarly men went to sleep.

Then the tribe behind arrived. A wave of stubby limbs rolled over Preacher. Someone snatched his sap away and used it. His aim was erratic. Gnarly men suffered more often than Preacher.

Then darkness enveloped Preacher.

Four gnarly men stood over him, panting and rubbing bruises. Their leader snarled, "Get the wagon. Get him out of here before the other one comes." He spoke a language of the far east, little-known in Shasesserre.

Another man, kneeling over the fallen, said, "Broken neck here, Emerald."

The leader, Emerald, indistinguishable from the others, cursed the dead man for complicating his life. "Throw him in the wagon, too." He kicked Preacher.

Soup—so called since childhood, for reasons he no longer recalled—became suspicious. His quarry was not trying hard enough to escape. When there was no Preacher waiting, and the gnarly man turned into Bleek Alley, he knew.

Soup trotted back the way he had come.

Soup carried no weapon but the knife he used when eating. He did not approve of bloody-minded violence— not to mention that Shasesserre had laws banning civilians carrying blades—though he was not shy about mixing it up when the occasion arose. None of Rider's gang were.

He stopped at a smithy, bought a pick, left its head with the baffled toolmaker.

He repaired to the mouth of Bleek Alley, listened, heard the distant creak of wagon wheels. Of Preacher there was no sign. "Trouble for sure," he muttered, and stalked into the shadows.

Trouble did not disappoint him. There was a sudden rush of feet. He hoisted his pick handle and used it like a two-handed sword.

Its heavy end tapped skulls. Gnarly men shrieked. Heads cracked like eggshells. Bones broke. Soup let out a wild howl. "Who ambushed who?" he laughed, and laid on again.

Emerald saw the way of things early. He fell back, scrambled up onto a rusted metal balcony dangling precariously eight feet above, yelled at his men to flee. As Soup passed below, shouting, "Stand and take it, you cowards!" Emerald reached down and whacked the back of his head. Soup's lights went out. Moments later he was bound and in the wagon with Preacher and several dead gnarly men.

IV

Rider went up the tower with a tireless ease matched only by Su-Cha, who levitated from stage to stage. The imp grinned down at Chaz, Spud, and Greystone, offering endless unsolicited advice.

Chaz threatened, "Any more mouth and we'll see how you rope dive without a rope." It was an empty threat. Su-Cha would fall only if he wanted.

Rider reached the high platform well ahead of his men. Below, people pointed and asked what the Protector's son was doing. He was well-known, which he did not like. It would interfere with his new work.

The side of the platform facing the Golden Crescent boasted a pair of lithe, springy fifty-foot poles of newly trimmed green wood brought up just that morning. Workmen were attaching long, tough, elastic ropes. Similar poles and ropes were installed at stages all up the tower. Later, Shasesserre's young men would place their ankles in harnesses attached to those ropes and dive into space. The springy poles would absorb their momentum and halt them just short of death. They would dive from ever higher stations, their numbers dwindling as altitude betrayed courage's limit. It would be dark before they reached the top. The remaining divers would jump carrying torches. Rider had won the competition during his sixteenth, seventeenth, and eighteenth years.

He glanced at the workmen, then paid them no mind. They showed more interest in him. He was a remarkable physical specimen, and a reputed genius.

The death engine stood at the side of the platform facing the Citadel. Rider asked, "Anyone touched this?"

Heads shook. One man offered, "We didn't know what it was for. What is it?"

Rider ignored the question. "Ingenious." He moved around the engine cautiously, never touching it.

"Geep!" a workman said.

"Hello to you, too," Su-Cha singsonged.

Rider faced his associates. "Look this thing over when you catch your breath, Spud. See if it's booby-trapped."

"Never again," Spud gasped. "Never again." He began studying the machine.

"You still got to get down," Chaz reminded.

"Let him jump," Su-Cha said. "Maybe he can knit wings before he hits."

"Your sense of humor is juvenile," Chaz observed.

"I'm just a young thing. Barely two thousand."

"No booby traps," Spud announced.

"Do you recognize the workmanship?"

"No." Spud looked over the edge. He swayed. Rider grabbed his arm.

"Dang!" Su-Cha said. "Thought he'd try it."

Chaz kicked toward the imp's behind. Su-Cha was absent when his foot arrived. He cackled from a far corner of the platform, perched atop a workman's tool chest.

Mumbling, the workmen started leaving.

"Let's see if my father marked his killer. Su-Cha, do you smell anything?"

The imp sniffed around the killing machine. His face puckered into one huge frown. "It's there. But weak. Be hard to isolate." He got down on all fours, snuffled like a hound. He went right to the top of the ladder and over the side, head down.

"Don't take no demon to figure that," Chaz said. "No murderer was going to fly out of here."

Greystone suggested, "We could offer a reward for witnesses." The scholar seldom spoke. When he did, even Rider listened. "Even at midnight someone might have seen him."

"Hmm. No," Rider said. "Not yet. Likely to raise questions. Maybe if the news gets out. You and Spud might visit neighborhood watering holes. If anybody did see a climber he'll talk about it."

Spud complained, "Come on, Rider. Why can't we go with you? How come Chaz and Su-Cha get in on all the excitement?"

"Chaz will miss out, too. He'll be looking for Soup and Preacher. We should have heard from them." Rider slowly turned as he spoke, flicked a glance toward the Citadel. "Ah. I thought so."

"What?" Chaz demanded.

"Someone is in the lab. Thought I saw movement a while ago."

"Let's go!" Chaz whooped, and went over the side. Spud and Greystone followed. Rider examined the death machine again, then seized one of the diving ropes.

He jumped.

Workmen yelled. Rider plunged toward the Plaza. The spring in rope and pole absorbed his momentum. He came to a halt six feet from the surface, let go, landed running. His associates were not yet thirty feet down from the tower platform.

He whipped into the Citadel, climbed stairs at a pace punishing even for his iron muscles, slammed into his father's laboratory.

The place was a shambles.

He placed one finger on the wall. It was warm. He nodded, made supple-fingered passes over the floor. Glimmering footprints appeared. Two men. One larger than the other. The larger tracks ran to the window and back. A lookout. The smaller feet went straight to the door, spacing indicating haste. The lookout had witnessed Rider's jump.

Rider was rereading his father's message when Chaz, Omar, Greystone, and Su-Cha arrived. "Catch them, Rider?" the imp piped.

"No. They were looking for a last message. And found one."

"Darn. That means trouble."

"For them." Rider indicated the wall.

Su-Cha chortled. "You changed it. Are they going to be mad."

"More than you know. I'll be there to greet them."

Chaz rubbed his hands together eagerly, drew the huge and entirely illegal sword he carried. He examined its edge.

"No," Rider said. "I'm going alone. You have your assignments."

"Rider!"

Rider ignored their protests, leaned out the window.

"What is it?" The whole laboratory shivered. Glass rattled. Dust danced.

"Military airship. I should have sensed it sooner. The web is more damaged than I thought. We'll have to wrap this up fast and get to repairing it."

Noise rose from the Plaza as the airship passed over. It settled toward the military moorings on the

Martial Fields.

It was a gaudy bombard from the eastern fleet. The side effects of the sorcery that propelled it faded.

"Off on your errands now," Rider said.

"Suppose we catch the killer?" Su-Cha asked.

"Bring him here." Rider's voice was cold grey iron. "There are questions I want to ask."

"Right."

Chaz was out the door already, humming. He'd thought of an amusing trick to play on Soup and Preacher.

Su-Cha, Spud, and Greystone followed.

Rider busied himself in the laboratory, collecting items he concealed about himself. Then he set out on the trail of glowing footprints. He believed he knew where they were headed, but wanted to see what stops they made.

The footprints materialized a dozen steps ahead of him, faded that far behind. Before long the men making them separated. He elected to follow the smaller prints.

V

Chance led Su-Cha, Spud, and Greystone across Chaz's path. The northerner was holding up a wall with one shoulder while talking to an attractive young woman. His mind was not on business.

Su-Cha said, "Feast your glims on this, guys," and he scrunched his eyes tight shut.

His body changed. Not much, but enough to provide the appearance of a child about four. Then he charged Chaz, wrapped his arms around the barbarian's legs. "Daddy. Daddy. Mommy says you have to come right home."

Chaz's jaw dropped. The woman's brow wrinkled. The barbarian saw Spud and Greystone grinning. He roared, "Su-Cha! I'll flay you and use your damned spook hide..."

"Daddy? Are you mad?"

Chaz kicked the imp into traffic, where he narrowly missed being trampled.

The young woman gave him bloody hell. He tried to explain. She did not believe a word he said. Imps!

Chaz was angry. He did not observe his surroundings in the alert way survival in the north demanded. He overlooked the gnarly men entirely, though they stood out even among the ten thousand outrageous foreigners haunting that Shasesserren street.

He worked his way from place to place, asking after Soup and Preacher. None of their acquaintances had seen them. He grew concerned. They should not have been so hard to find.

He made the acquaintance of the gnarly men as he cut through a delivery way between major streets. Those men seemed to prefer alleyways.

A rush of feet from behind.

Chaz's reactions were not impaired. Out came the illegal but seldom challenged sword. A gnarly man howled out his life as a cross stroke opened his belly. Another shrieked and clutched a savaged bicep. The mob halted, danced back out of reach.

Emerald cursed his men for idiots, cursed himself for being saddled with them, cursed the orders that brought him to Shasesserre. He redeployed. Two men with gladiatorial-style nets moved to the fore.

Chaz was not given to suicidal heroics. He retreated.

The net men knew their stuff. They feinted, pressed, feinted, tried to tangle Chaz's legs and blade. Their comrades threw brickbats. One especially savage throw glanced off Chaz's shin and succeeded in distracting him.

Net in high, brushed aside. But the net low tangled his right ankle. Down he went. The pack leaped forward. Chaz bellowed and roared, punched, kicked, and bit. He littered that alley with howling villains. But all the while Emerald danced in and out, whapping his hard northern head with the captured sap.

Chaz gave up to the darkness.

Soup wakened to a world throbbing and fogged. At one moment it seemed he was in a darkened coliseum, its walls so distant they were invisible, the lamps starry pinpricks miles away. The next moment it all rushed in. He was near crushed by gaudy eastern furnishings impossible to enumerate. His limited attention focused on a single detail, a slim, golden-skinned woman of incredible beauty, who paced before a wallhanging embroidered with eastern fantasies.

She was a little thing, and young, but no child. She moved with an animal litheness that set Soup's brain more aspin.

She said something softly.

A muffled male voice replied. Soup could not distinguish individual words. But it seemed a voice he should know.

The woman glanced at the prisoners. She had the

most remarkable eyes Soup had ever seen. Big, green, they were eyes to swallow a man's soul. She was a trap to break a heart of stone!

She faced left. "There is no point complaining. Emerald is not here. And no change in plan can be made before the Master arrives."

The male voice became more strident but no more clear. Soup wished for a glimpse of the speaker.

The woman replied, "Your desires are of consequence only insofar as they complement those of the Master."

More male talk, angry. Threatening.

The woman smiled. She pointed. "Do you wish to join them? Or to do the Master's bidding?"

The complaints subsided.

All this while Soup's world shrank and swelled and rolled on its belly and back. Now darkness returned.

Later the veil parted again. A large, fluffy cat was nosing around his face. It would not go away.

A different male voice grumbled something in an eastern tongue. Many feet tramped. Men grunted. A body flopped down nearby. A gnarly man bent over it, forced something small and brown between slack lips.

Chaz!

Another of the group taken. What was going on?

The woman said, "Emerald, our friend doesn't like the way we're doing this. We're not moving fast enough to suit him."

The gnarly man spat. "I came here with twelve men, as you asked, friend. I have five dead and two with broken bones already. You were not honest with us. I think, when the Master arrives, you will answer for that."

The unknown man responded with fear in his muffled voice.

The woman said, "Your plan is sound. It will be pursued. We will isolate the Protector's son from his friends, then handle him. Then we will eliminate others who would resist us. That will not be difficult once the Master arrives."

The Master. The Master, Soup thought. *Who is that?*

Emerald said, "I suggest you obtain local helpers. I cannot keep losing men."

There was a stir. Someone came to where Soup, Preacher, and Chaz lay. He wore a heavy papier-mâché mask pierced by two narrow eyeslits. The man in the mask laughed. "For this I will hire an army. I must have them all."

Soup again thought he sensed something familiar.

"Go recruit, then," Emerald said.

The man in the mask went away.

Emerald and the golden-skinned woman murmured to one another. Soup's universe remained unstable. And now his head hurt terribly. Preacher, he noted, showed signs of recovering, too. Chaz, though, was out for the count.

Then he went down into the darkness again.

He wakened to: "The Master comes!" The golden-skinned woman's breath caught in her throat. A fetching effect, he thought... The dizzies caught and spun him around.

He was not sure what he saw next was not part of a drug dream. A hideous little man no bigger than Su-Cha, with a large normal head, stood peering down at him. His coloring and dress were oriental. His hands were folded before him. His fingers were encased in golden shields meant to protect nails grown many inches long.

The dwarf radiated malevolence.

The Master.

The golden-skinned woman lay face down behind him, abasing herself. Of Emerald there was no sign.

Emerald was stalking the remainder of Rider's men.

His manpower depleted, he had opted for cunning. He posted his men, then sought out Spud, Greystone, and Su-Cha. Speaking Shasesserren brokenly, bowing, he blocked their path. "Is told you fella seek holy joe fella Pleacher, so? Is bounty find same?"

"Maybe," Spud said. "Depends."

"You come see belong you fella fliend Pleacher, longside tlouble." Emerald hurried away.

The three followed. "A remarkable physical specimen," Greystone said, scholarly curiosity piqued.

Spud grumbled, "There's an accent behind that pidgin that I know from somewhere. Can't get my hooks on it."

Grinning, prancing ahead, back to the gnarly man, Su-Cha said, "We've found our man. This is the guy Rider's old man marked."

Spud and Greystone halted. "You mean?…"

"Yes indeed." Su-Cha's little round face went hard.

"You fella come?"

"By all means," Greystone replied. "By all means."

"Ambush of some kind," Spud decided.

"Somebody's going to ambush somebody," Su-Cha chirped.

But they were not prepared when it happened, as, passing a tavern, they were set upon by five gnarly men with nets and ropes. It was no fight at all. Greystone and Spud were netted, tied, and dragged into an alley almost before bystanders were aware something was happening.

Su-Cha was another matter. The gnarly men could not keep a net on a creature able to discorporate and reintegrate elsewhere. But they produced fetishes of holly and garlic and a rope of silver. They surrounded him with the rope. He could not escape their closing circle. The holly and garlic prevented him getting close enough to strike back.

Grinning, Emerald tossed a net into which silver thread had been plaited.

The last of Rider's associates was caught.

"Better this time," Emerald said. "Let's deliver them. Then we try the tough one."

"These guys were tough enough," one man protested.

"We'll have help after this. Shut up and come on. People are getting nosey."

VI

Rider followed the glowing footprints to a grand mansion on the Balajka Hill, Shasesserre's wealthiest section. He faced a decision. The tracks went in, but then came out again. Continue following them? Or investigate the house?

That was supposed to be empty.

Jehrke had known all Shasesserre's leading men, so his son knew them, too. This mansion belonged to one Vlazos, currently posted to the western army for his year in five of public service.

Someone had usurped the place in his absence.

Rider decided he would come back later. He continued tracking the man who had had his father murdered.

He was two hundred yards away when a rushing coach nearly overran him. He rose angrily. Such drivers had no place in Shasesserre on the overcrowded streets. The coach turned in through the gate to the Vlazos mansion.

Rider intuited the arrival of an important conspirator. Perhaps one more important than the man he tracked. He turned back.

The Vlazos grounds were surrounded by a fifteen-foot wall. Rider made sure no one was in sight, swarmed up using cracks between stones for foot-and handholds. He peeped over the top, saw nothing remarkable, hoisted himself, dropped lightly to the manicured turf inside. He reached the side of the house only moments after the front door closed behind the newcomer.

The carriage stood untended. Rider sent his wizard-trained senses to explore. He could find no guard behind the door. The newcomer and his driver were moving deeper into the house, one toward the kitchens, the other toward where several lifesparks glimmered.

He recognized the sparks of Preacher, Chaz, Soup.

The conclusion was unavoidable. His father's enemies had made them prisoners.

Rider went through the door as silently as death. He followed the man who had come in the coach. Already his driver was in the kitchens, drinking. Soon Rider heard a piping voice say something unintelligible.

A dozen steps more, along a shadowed hallway. He noted that oriental furnishings had replaced those Vlazos preferred. Ahead, a strong smell of rare eastern incense. A tapestry hung across a large doorway. He heard movement beyond it.

Rider peeped through the narrowest of gaps on one side. He saw his three men immediately, bound and unconscious. Nearer him, an attractive oriental woman abased herself upon the floor. She chattered in a melodic tongue.

Rider spoke half a hundred languages, but this one evaded him.

The newcomer spoke one curt syllable. Rider nearly jumped. The man was right in front of him. Was he invisible? His gaze dropped. A dwarf!

He hearkened back to tales his father had told, in his uncertain, fragmentary fashion. There were many old enemies. One was an especially nasty dwarf. What was that name? Yes. Kralj Odehnal.

Kralj Odehnal, renowned sorcerer and dreaded torturer. One of the villains long stifled by the Protector. But Odehnal was a loner.

The dwarf and young woman chattered at one another. The fate of Rider's men was being determined. He prepared to surprise their captors.

But, it seemed, they were to be spared a while. He supposed as potential leverage. He decided to await developments. There was more afoot than a murder plot.

Time passed. Then men trooped in through another entrance. They carried Spud, Greystone, and Su-Cha.

Su-Cha! Even the imp.

His father's enemies were wasting no time bringing the shadow to Shasesserre.

It was time to move. To break the conspiracy's back before it became aware it had been found out.

Rider took an ebony figurine from a hidden pocket, held it against his forehead, over the point called the third eye. After a moment of concentration, he spat on it.

Beyond the tapestry the dwarf and gnarly men gabbled at one another in the unfamiliar language. Rider ripped the hanging aside, tossed the figurine, shouted, "Pyznar, you live!"

A shadow exploded into a dark, tusked demon. Its fangy mouth opened in a silent roar. Men squealed and shrieked. The sudden monster jumped on one of Emerald's gang. The dwarf cursed. The woman fled instantly, without thought or hesitation.

The shadow turned on a second victim as Rider stepped past the tapestry, his hands afire with fresh sorcery. Odehnal looked at him, snarled, "You!"

"Me. And the end of your game, Kralj." The shadow turned to a third gnarly man. Rider slapped his hands together, thrust them toward the dwarf. The combined fires flared violently, blindingly.

Odehnal shrieked, terrified, knowing he could muster no spell in time to save himself.

A gnarly man staggered into the space between Rider and Odehnal, shoved there by Emerald. The chief of the gnarly men snagged the dwarf and ran.

Rider's spell hit Emerald's sacrifice. Golden fires gnawed the man. He screamed. Then went silent when the shadow turned upon him.

Finished there, and with all Emerald's crew, the shadow faced Rider's men. It took Rider a full minute to restore the demon to miniature form. By then he had abandoned hope of catching Odehnal. His task, now, was to get his men out before the dwarf struck back.

"Good show," Su-Cha congratulated, as Rider freed him first. The imp was the only one conscious.

"Help get these guys untied. We have to get them out. This place will be under attack in a few minutes."

Su-Cha moved. He knew Rider wasted no threats. "Who were those guys?"

"The dwarf is Kralj Odehnal. A sorcerer. An old enemy of my father. It can't be coincidence that he turned up as soon as the web began to fray."

Soup proved to be conscious. When Rider removed his gag, he croaked, "The runt's the mastermind, Rider. But there's somebody from the Citadel involved. He came up with the original plan. He got the runt in. Then *he* took over. They were going to wipe out a lot of people besides us."

"Uhm," Rider responded. "If you can walk, get out. Help Preacher." Rider hoisted Spud and Greystone effortlessly, ran to the nearest exit, out onto the lawn, dumped the two men, was back for Chaz in seconds.

The house had begun to glow when he charged out with the barbarian. The glow grew into a blinding brilliance. The roar of collapsing masonry rose inside the brightness.

Rider never looked. He dropped Chaz by Su-Cha. "When they recover, go to the laboratory. Wait for me there." Before Su-Cha could protest he spun and ran to the gate.

The street showed no sign of Odehnal or his coach.

Rider shrugged, took up the trail of glowing footprints once more. Now he ran, a long, distance-devouring lope. Twice the trail led to and from the homes of men high in imperial councils. Rider did not pause. He would get back to those men later.

Then the trail turned the direction he expected.

Rider's teeth showed in a grim smile.

VII

Emerald did his bandy-legged best to keep pace with Rider while remaining unnoticed. He failed. He was built for endurance. Of speed he was capable only of short bursts. He turned back, watched the crowd gathering to stare at the wreckage of the Vlazos mansion. In time Rider's gang came out the gate, supporting one another. He trailed them. His heart thumped wildly whenever he reflected on the fact that thirteen men had come to Shasesserre. He was the last one left, and only the Protector himself had been dispatched.

The Master might be in for as much trouble with the son as he had had with the father. Maybe more. They said the Protector trained his child from birth to assume the role he now faced.

He had to seize it first, though!

Right to the Citadel. Just as expected. Emerald blended into the holiday crowd in the Plaza. The initial festivities had begun. He pretended interest till he was sure he saw movement behind the window of the Protector's laboratory. Then he went to report to the Master.

Rider's men picked up and cleaned up. "Looks like a whole tribe of northmen camped here a week," Preacher grumbled, adding some scriptural quote about the savages bringing the earth low.

"Why do you always accuse us?"

"Because civilized people…"

Su-Cha, observing from the window, cackled.

Chaz glowered his way. "I haven't forgotten you, devil. Your time is coming. Stewed imp with a garlic garnish. Think about it. Wonder when you're going into the pot."

Spud said, "If you ask me it would be revenge enough just getting him to help here. He wouldn't do his share if…"

"Hold it," Su-Cha said, in a tone suddenly serious. "Take a look at this." He dropped off the sill, stood looking over with his chin resting on his forearms, childlike.

Chaz and Preacher joined him. Cautiously.

"It's that villain, Emerald," Preacher said.

The festivities were gathering momentum. The Plaza was crowded. Nevertheless, Emerald stood out. He was on the fringe of the mob, watching the Citadel gate.

The entire band crowded the window now. "Let's get him," Spud said.

"Rider said stay here," Greystone countered. "The web needs mending. He'll want our help."

"But he'd want us to do something if we saw that guy."

"We should stay put," Chaz said, surprising everyone. Usually Chaz was the first to yield to impulse, the most eager to jump into trouble.

"This mess is *big*," he said defensively. "We need to get organized to handle it."

Su-Cha declared, "I don't need to be organized to dance on that thug's head. And this time he isn't going to slick me." The imp headed for the door. Everyone but Chaz and Greystone followed.

Chaz went to the window to watch the gnarly man. Greystone continued picking up. He said, "Precipitous action often leads to its own reward. The sensible course is to restore the web before undertaking any action. We need its support."

"You figure the news is out yet?" Chaz glanced at the grisly ornament still pinned to the wall.

"This cabal would have an interest in maintaining secrecy till they placed themselves in the most favorable position."

"What happens tonight?"

"What do you mean?"

"Jehrke always hands out the prizes to the rope divers."

"Ah. Yes. So. These enemies of ours must have been confident they could achieve their ends before then."

"Rider will take his father's place, I guess. Oh-oh. There they go."

Greystone joined Chaz. They watched their comrades race toward the gnarly man, who spotted them, took off, stubby bowlegs pumping furiously. "That fellow can surely run."

"For a ways," Chaz said. "Bet he ain't much over a quarter mile." Below, Soup suddenly slowed to a trot, though he did not give up pursuit. "What's Soup up to?"

Soup had been smitten by a suspicion that Emerald had been too easily spotted. Maybe he was leading them into another ambush. If so, he would get a surprise of his own. Soup would materialize after the trap was sprung.

Emerald began to slow and his pursuers to gain. The looks he cast back seemed genuinely desperate. He whirled around a corner, knobby limbs flailing.

Rider's men rounded the corner and drifted to a halt. "Where'd he go?" Spud demanded. "He couldn't disappear into thin air."

"Look around," Preacher said.

"I know. 'Seek and ye shall find.' Su-Cha, do your stuff."

There was no place for the gnarly man to have gone. The street was just a wide alleyway between two doorless walls. It dead-ended in another brick wall.

"Dig through that trash," Soup said. "Maybe he's under it." He had arrived to find his friends baffled.

The usually loquacious Su-Cha said nothing for several minutes. Then he grunted, snatched up a broken brick, flung it at the alley-spanning wall. It did not rebound. It simply vanished.

Soup howled. "We've been hornswoggled! The wall is an illusion."

He charged forward—and through. His hair stood up and crackled. When he looked back he saw no evidence of the illusory wall, just his comrades looking baffled.

There was no sign of Emerald.

The others joined him. "What now?" Spud asked.

"We still have a trick," Su-Cha said. He grinned and tapped his nose.

The others chuckled. "Is he going to be surprised."

Soup, though, recalled his earlier reservations. "He may be leading us away from the laboratory."

"Maybe," Spud admitted. "But Chaz and Greystone are there. And he expected to lose us here. Let's go, imp."

There was a delicate tap at the laboratory door. Chaz and Greystone exchanged looks. Greystone whispered, "I'll cover," and stepped into a contrivance of mirrors from which a man could watch the doorway without being seen. He picked up a light crossbow.

The tapping was repeated.

Chaz pulled the door inward.

His eyes grew huge. He gasped, "I think I'm in love. The heavens have opened and shed an angel on my doorstep."

The woman was startled, not just by this remark but by the barbarian's size. Then she glanced over her shoulder fearfully, as if expecting peril to overtake her any moment. "May I come in?" she asked breathlessly.

"A godsend," Chaz said. "I have to be dreaming. Do come in. Do sit down. Just anywhere."

The woman did so, her gaze fixing upon the cadaver of Protector Jehrke. Her mouth opened and closed several times. Nothing came out. Horror flooded her face.

"More like a devil in disguise," Greystone said, stepping out of the mirror contraption. "This is the witch Soup told us about."

"Mercy," Chaz breathed, startled. "It isn't possible. The gods could not be so cruel as to make something so gorgeous so wicked."

"Horsefeathers," Greystone countered. He prided himself on his immunity to the glamor and wiles of the fair sex. "Bet that Emerald character was supposed to draw us off so she could get in here and unravel what's left of the web." The scholar kept his weapon aimed at the woman's heart.

Chaz was smitten but not blind. "Well? What about it, Sweetheart?"

"The Master planned that. But not I. I knew you would not all pursue Emerald. Your reputations say you are too wise."

Greystone snorted and muttered.

The woman continued, "I hoped to be captured."

"Why?" Greystone demanded.

"Because that is the only way I will ever escape him."

Chaz drifted to the window. Below, the festivities were approaching a roar. The rope divers had begun jumping. He saw nothing alarming. He moved to the doorway, checked the hall. Nothing. From a shelf nearby he took an earthen jar, scattered part of its contents outside. Tiny seeds rolled around. He stomped one. It exploded with a loud pop. "Good enough." He closed and locked the door.

"Tell your story, Sister," Greystone said. His crossbow remained unwavering. "I haven't heard a good fairy tale in years."

"Kralj Odehnal—the sorcerer who had you captured, and would have had you killed had he taken Ride-Master Jehrke into his power…"

"We know all that. We want to know about you. Who are you?"

"Easy, Greystone," Chaz said. "Would you care for something to drink, sweet lady?"

The woman glanced at the remains of the Protector. "I couldn't."

"Going to have to do something about him," Chaz muttered. "Starting to spook me, hanging there. Like he was watching everything we do."

"Tell your story," Greystone snapped.

"I am Caracené, a slave of Kralj Odehnal, who is known to his creatures as the Master. I was given to him as part payment for his joining the scheme to destroy Protector Jehrke and unseat Shasesserre as mistress of the world."

She was no Shasesserren, nor had her like appeared among the City's slaves. At least openly. Such beauty was too rare and precious to be allowed public display. Nor did she dress as, or have the manner of, a slave. Those eyes... She was a slave-taker.

Puzzled, Chaz asked, "Who gave you to him?" He found that name Odehnal vaguely familiar. He could not imagine anyone bribing such a monster.

The woman stared at the cadaver on the wall. "I cannot say. One greater than he. One from whom none escape."

"Horsefeathers," Greystone said again. "We're being stalled, Chaz. It's time for a truth-casting. I'm no sorcerer, but I can manage that much."

The woman bolted to her feet. "No! It would kill me! I must go. I was wrong to come here. There is no hope here, either." She looked at the dead Protector once more. "Not even *he*..."

Chaz moved to comfort her. As he reached out, a loud *pop! pop! pop!* came from beyond the door.

The woman gasped, "He knows I thought to betray him!"

Greystone jerked his crossbow irritably, indicating that she should retreat into the connecting library. Chaz moved to a peephole that, through a succession of mirrors, would show him who was outside without his having to reveal himself.

VIII

Rider slowed his pace after he had run three miles. Not that he was exhausted. He'd barely worked up a sweat. He ran ten miles every morning. But the tracks he followed were increasingly fresh. He did not want to overtake his man here, between the piers and yards and warehouses and ways of the Golden Crescent, and the strip of ten thousand markets the great ships served. There were crowds like no other city ever boasted. This was the hub of world trade, where the quarters of the earth came together in a frenzy and babble. Here there was no privacy, ever.

Rider's mouth was set in a grim smile. No doubt about it. His father's killer was headed into the trap prepared.

He stopped to purchase a quart of juice and a meat pasty. There had been no time to eat before. When he estimated time enough had passed, he washed at a public fountain, then strode toward the airship yards.

None but guards were on duty there, for it was a public holiday. The gatemen knew him, waved him through. He strode between vast construction docks, mooring stays, gas works where Jehrke's apprentices produced the magical air that buoyed the ships of the sky. All this vast industry was his father's doing. His greatest legacy to the City, perhaps, for it would go on even if his peace failed to persevere. The secrets here would be the first plunder sought by Shasesserre's enemies.

Thus, Rider had altered his father's message, knowing his murderer would believe the airship yards the likeliest place for the Protector to hide something.

The nethermost part of the yards occupied a promontory overlooking the Golden Crescent, the miles of waterfront facing the Bridge of the World, that long, narrow, snaking channel connecting the Amor Ocean with the Middle Sea. The ruin of an ancient watchtower stood at the headland's tip. Around it were structures of recent vintage, the Protector's original and now personal shipyard. As Rider approached he saw his father's ships protruding from their cradles like the brightly colored humped backs of whales breaking the surface of a flotsam-strewn sea. Twelve of them, in a variety of shapes and sizes. The family wealth.

The Jehrke yards were more still than the greater yards around them. Here even the guards were on holiday.

A shadow fell across Rider's path. He looked up at the four-hundred-foot mast which rose beside the ruined watchtower. In his youth, in rare moments when he was free of studies, he had climbed that tower and watched the parti-colored sails scud along the Bridge, outward bound or coming home. So often he had longed to fly away upon those canvas wings, to lands of adventure... There was adventure enough now. And a lifetime's worth to come.

He entered the vast, long, hollow building where airships were brought out of the weather, making

not a sound. He listened. Seconds later there was a
pop, like a dry branch breaking, from far down the
building. A startled exclamation, then curses, echoed
off the empty walls.

Rider began walking, making no effort to keep his
heels from clicking on the polished stone floor.

The cursing ceased. It was followed by a rustling,
like that of frantic rats in a wall. As Rider neared the
doorway beyond which his quarry waited, he heard a
sob of frustration.

He stepped through the doorway into what had
been his father's shipyard office.

The man caught there, one hand inside a desk that
refused to let him go, was not surprised to see him. He
had a dagger in his left hand.

"Vlazos!" Rider said, startled. "I thought you were
with the army in Kleyvorn."

Vlazos said nothing.

Rider pulled up a chair. "It does come together,
though."

Vlazos hammered the desk with his dagger.

"Tell me about it," Rider said. He stared hard at his
captive, his gaze like that of the fabled snake. He made a
gesture with his left hand, caught Vlazos' gaze and held
it. Vlazos' mouth opened and closed like that of a guppy
as he fought a compulsion to betray his confederates.
"Tell me who else is participating in this atrocity."

Rider took several measured breaths, counting.
His anger threatened to overwhelm him. He could
not comprehend why a man of Vlazos' status would
betray Shasesserre for personal gain.

Rider's spell took the inhibitions off the telling of
the truth. He used it sparingly, for societies are founded

upon mutually shared self-deceptions. But in Vlazos' case the spell opened no floodgate. Had the man acted from idealistic, if misguided, motives, he would have defended himself.

Silence, too, is a telling of truth. Greed and powerlust were the foundation stones of the conspiracy threatening Shasesserre's peace.

"Where, besides your mansion, has your cabal set up?" Rider demanded. "Who belongs?"

Vlazos was under the spell fully now. He began naming names, most of them ones Rider expected. They were men who obstructed the Protector at every turn. "And Kralj Odehnal? How did he become involved?"

Vlazos' breath caught in his throat. He gobbled, and scratched at his neck. His face puffed and darkened. His eyes grew huge. He was strangling on sorcery.

Rider heard someone move in the great space outside. He did not turn, for he was trying to find the end of the spell killing Vlazos, to unravel it before the man suffocated. He could not... Vlazos got out one whimper before life abandoned him.

Rider rose. "Shy key?" he murmured. "What would that mean?"

He rushed out of the office. Nothing stirred within the cavernous building. But the far door, through which he himself had entered, stood ajar. It leaked a pane of light. He had not left it that way.

Rider reached it in a time that would have shamed most athletes. He paused before stepping outside, every sense probing for signs of an ambush.

He detected only the fading disturbance of the powerful cycle of magicks that propelled airships.

"Feeble and high-pitched," he murmured. "A small ship driven by someone self-taught." He stepped into the glare of day, caught a glimpse of an airship hurrying down the Golden Crescent, flying low.

He thought about taking one of his father's small ships in pursuit. But none were ready. It would take an hour to charge one with gas. The murderer of his father's murderer was safely away.

He went back and searched Vlazos. There was nothing of interest on the man except a key of the sort which fit the safe chests at the Imperial Treasury. He pocketed it.

He found no satisfaction in the fact that his father's killer had himself been slain. Vlazos set the wheel rolling, but now it was Odehnal's toy.

Where had the dwarf learned the spells to move an airship? How? That complex was a closely guarded secret, taught only to men whom Jehrke trusted absolutely.

Rider strolled toward the Citadel. The sun was into its westward plunge. About time he sought an audience with the King. The man needed to know, to prepare for the storm. And Rider hoped for his blessing in his assumption of the Protector's role.

He decided he'd better get himself a chariot. All this walking and running—even he was subject to cumulative fatigue.

But first, before anything—even before seeing the King—he had to restore the web. When an enemy could bring a pirate airship within a few hundred yards undetected, the situation was desperate.

Just how tired he had become, and thus unalert, was demonstrated when he reached his father's laboratory.

He failed to notice the pop seeds scattered in the hall. His feet stirred a rapid-fire racket.

The door swung inward. "Rider!" Chaz said. "We've got company."

He saw the golden-skinned woman in the doorway to the library. She saw him for the first time. Her eyes widened.

"You catch him?" Greystone asked.

"Yes. It was Vlazos."

"And?"

"He died before he could say much."

"Oh."

Rider heard the hollow sound in Greystone's voice. "No. Not me. His confederates. With a strangulation spell. They fled in an airship."

Greystone looked properly astounded.

"Yes. First order of business now is to restore the web. Where are the others?"

Chaz explained about Emerald.

"I told them to stay here. Well. I suppose they have to learn the hard way."

IX

Emerald shambled along with his hands in his pockets, grinning and whistling. He had made clowns of those guys again. Too bad he had not had men enough to ambush them. Ten or fifteen guys with crossbows waiting behind the illusory wall. They wouldn't have known what hit them. But he had no men now, because the Master and that Vlazos fool insisted Rider's gang be taken alive. That damned Vlazos better find some local talent.

Someone stepped into his path. Emerald halted, lifted his gaze... and squawked.

Preacher grinned.

Emerald looked around wildly.

The other three closed in. Spud was next nearest, about twenty feet away, popping a fist into a palm meaningfully.

The gnarly man was *quick!* Preacher just had time for a startled squeak. Then he was in the air, flailing toward Spud. Emerald put on speed. More than a touch of panic drove him. He did not know what to do. There was no provision in the plan for his not being able to shake his pursuers. The wall of illusion should have worked.

It was a failed plan anyway. Not all Rider's men had left the Citadel.

The Master would know what to do. But he could not run to the Master. That would lead these men to him.

He grimaced. Then grinned. He would lead them away from the Master. Wear them down, till the Master became disturbed by his failure to report and investigated.

Soup gasped, "Are we going to keep this up all day? Or are we going to catch him?" He stopped at a chandler's shop. The others paused. As long as Su-Cha could sniff Emerald's trail they would not lose him. "Let's get organized. He isn't going to lead us anywhere. If he gets too tired and scared he might try picking us off. We've got to capture him."

"How you figure on doing that?" Su-Cha demanded. "Preacher and Spud already blew it."

"Buy some rope. Rope him like a steer, bind him up, and carry him back to the Citadel."

Su-Cha cackled. "Great. Get it! Reams or bales or bundles or whatever rope comes in. A mile of it! We'll turn him into a human cocoon."

Three minutes later they were on the trail again, armed with coils of light line. Fifteen minutes later they had Emerald surrounded.

The gnarly man saw their intent. He darted this way and that. A wicked knife sprang into his hand. He feinted toward Preacher, rushed Spud.

Hands and feet flashed. The knife flickered away. Spud and Emerald rolled over and over, grunting and yelling. Su-Cha pranced around them, trying to slip a noose over Emerald's head. Soup got one on an ankle and pulled.

Preacher looped an arm, took off. Emerald stretched out, cursing and flailing. Spud thumped his head a few times. Soup got another rope on. The four of them began baling the gnarly man.

All this took place on a busy street. Passersby pretended blindness. Shasesserre was that kind of city still, centuries after Jehrke began trying to turn it around.

"Hi ho, hi ho," Soup laughed as he and Spud hoisted their prisoner. "Off to gaol for you, friend. Let's somebody find a wagon. This sucker's pants are full of lead."

Preacher hired a rickshaw. Emerald rode. The others ran alongside, laughing and clowning.

Chaz answered the laboratory door. He grinned when he saw Emerald, but held a finger to his lips. "Keep it down. Rider is mending the web."

Soup and Preacher plopped Emerald down under the open window, where he could look at the Protector and contemplate his fate. They joined the crowd in the library, where Rider had spread his father's extra web charts atop a table fifteen feet long and five wide. Rider neither welcomed them nor upbraided them for leaving the Citadel. He gave them jobs to do.

Hours passed. The sun dropped to within two diameters of the horizon. The rope divers were just a few stages short of the tower's top. Rider finally rose, sighing wearily. "That's enough for now. We'll put the final touches on after we finish this business."

"Got you a present, Rider," Su-Cha crowed. He pranced around, made smoke come out his ears. "In the laboratory."

Rider followed the imp to the other room. Emerald sat where he had been dumped. "He's the one who did the deed," Su-Cha said. "It was him on the tower last night."

"Cool one," Chaz remarked. "If he can sleep now." Rider darted forward, afraid he had lost another prisoner. But Emerald *was* asleep. "There would have been a tug on the web," he told himself. He closed his eyes, allowed his being to flow out the web's strands, and the web to fill him. He sensed every magic within five miles of the Rock. Each was legitimate. He could detect nothing of Kralj Odehnal.

"Get the gag off him," Rider said. "Untie him. Let him get some circulation back. There's nowhere he can go."

Emerald cursed them roundly. He crawled to his feet, stood unsteadily. Then he spotted Caracené.

Unintelligible words whipped back and forth. They

got hot. Emerald was angry, accusing; Caracené bitter and defensive. Emerald became increasingly pale. He began to shake.

"Are you ready to talk to us?" Rider asked.

Emerald spat on the floor.

"I guess that means a truth-drawing. Greystone, Spud, set it up." Rider followed Emerald's gaze to his father's body. Something would have to be done.

"Hey!"

"Grab him!"

"Su-Cha!..."

Rider whirled as Emerald's feet went over the windowsill. The imp clung to one, desperately trying to catch Chaz's hand. He failed.

Emerald made not one sound as he plunged to his death.

Su-Cha, who was in no danger, did enough screeching for eight fall victims.

Rider elbowed his way to the window. He did not watch Emerald hit the Rock. He searched the Plaza for an island of reaction to Emerald's fall. He spied none. The gnarly man had done it on his own.

"Hey!" Greystone shouted. "The witch is getting away!"

Rider turned. Caracené had slipped out while they were distracted. His helpers rushed to the door. "Let her go," he said. "We can find her when we want."

"Huh?"

"Su-Cha?" Chaz asked.

"The web. I marked her while we were in the library. Greystone, you keep track. Maybe she'll run to Odehnal. The rest of you stay here. And stay alert. I'll be back in time to give out the rope-diving prizes."

"Where you going?" Soup asked.

"To see the King. Not a task I'll enjoy, I'm sure." As he departed he heard Chaz and Greystone pick up their argument about Caracené. Chaz was of the opinion that he was in love, and that Caracené was not unmoved by his own manly attributes. Greystone was of the opinion that Chaz had a head full of feathers. The others seconded his view.

X

"His Majesty is at dinner," a chamberlain told Rider. "Then he must prepare to join your father for the ceremonies. I suggest you return at a more normal time." He scowled blackly. Few men dared that with Ride-Master Jehrke.

"It's about the ceremonies. There's been a change of plan. I'm giving the medals in my father's stead."

The chamberlain's scowl deepened. "Even so. . ."

Rider glanced at the nearby guards. They fought smirks. Not everyone appreciated his family's special status.

"Meghan, I am tired, upset, and short on patience. I have to see the King. I'll walk through you or over you if you make me." Was the chamberlain part of the conspiracy? Doubtful. The man was doing his job as he saw it, with a touch of officious spite.

"What is the nature?. . ."

"If I wanted you to know I would have told you."

The chamberlain spun angrily, slammed a door in Rider's face. Rider was more irked with himself than with Meghan. He should not let his control slip like that. He stepped to the door, giving the guards a look that made them decide he was invisible. A tiny spell broke the bolt.

The King was a spare man in his thirties, tall and dark of hair and complexion, and new to the Shasesser-ren crown. His coffee eyes flashed fire as he shoved away from a table shared with two other men. Rider noted that both were trustworthy functionaries.

The King said, "This runs in the family. I tolerate your father's lack of manners and respect because he serves a purpose. But you're not Jehrke Victorious, Ride-Master. Tell me why you shouldn't be flogged out of here."

Rider's patience remained thin. "I'll give you two reasons. One is, I wouldn't let you. As my father would not. The other is that Jehrke is dead. I've taken over for him."

Absolute, deadly silence. Mouths worked but nothing came out.

"He was murdered before dawn, at the order of Khev Vlazos, by an assassin serving the sorcerer Kralj Odehnal. Vlazos, the assassin, and most of Odehnal's men have been dispatched. Odehnal remains at large, as do Vlazos' fellow conspirators. The web was damaged severely but has been restored. All is peaceful in Shasesserre—at the moment. I expect a wave of assassinations—reaching even the royal household—was planned for tonight. These attempts may go forward despite what I've done to inhibit Odehnal. End of report, except to note that an unlicensed airship is in the hands of the conspirators."

"Jehrke dead," one of the ministers breathed. "The gods forfend! Every barbarian on our borders will try to plunder the provinces."

The King noted, "We have more to fear from home-grown pillagers. They'll get the news first."

"What can we do?"

Rider said, "Do nothing. Nothing has changed except that I stand in my father's stead."

"Oh, no," the King countered. "Never again will any one man exercise that much power."

"Are you saying my father abused his?"

"Hardly. But…"

"He did tend to be a check on royal excess? Yes. I know. Though he seldom intervened even in your predecessors' blackest villainies."

The King glowered.

King Belledon was accounted a good ruler, but had held the throne only a year. Some of Shasesserre's most terrible monarchs had entered their reigns auspiciously.

"There will be no more Protector," the King said. "The office dies with the man."

Rider had anticipated this exchange. Good or evil, no monarch willingly accepted a potential check on his power. "There never was such an office. As you know. 'Protector' is an honorific bestowed by popular acclaim. No one appointed Jehrke. He did what was necessary for Shasesserre. As I will do. I have trained for the task since birth. I hope to achieve as much as Jehrke did."

The King went livid. "You defy me?"

Calmly, "Of course. As my father did you and every king before you." He raised a forestalling hand. "Save your outrage, your pride. Think about it when you're calm. Ask the people *their* wishes."

"The wishes of shopkeepers are of no consequence."

"That attitude is what makes shopkeepers and tradesmen hail a Jehrke Protector. I have done my duty to the state by giving warning. I'm going to get ready for the awards ceremony now."

The King stared at Rider, exasperated. "Like father, like son," he said. "Where are you going, Konstantin?"

"My people need to be alerted. I must tell…"

"No one. You will tell no one, on your life. Rider at least sees the ramifications of Jehrke's death, if he is so vain as to arrogate his father's place."

The other man present, a greyhair whose role was informal and advisory, said, "There should be no announcement. Let Rider take over. There will be speculation but slight inclination toward adventurism and chaos. A formal announcement would unleash the hounds of fear Jehrke kept chained."

The King grumbled something.

"You have your enemies, Belledon. Are they more restrained by the numbers of your soldiers or by the Protector's approval of your reign? Has any ruler he approved been found by an assassin? How many of the Bad Kings died natural deaths?"

"It *is* something to consider, Your Majesty," Konstantin observed.

The older man said, "You are a king, Belledon. Not a god. Never forget your oath. You serve Shasesserre. The City does not serve you."

The King continued to grumble, but admitted the truth. It was just such moments the old man was supposed to get him through.

Rider returned to his father's laboratory, thinking he had to get used to it being his. "Everyone's still here?"

he asked in mock surprise. "I'm amazed."

"Yeah," Chaz grumbled.

Spud said, "Rider, have you decided what to do about your father? Can't put it off much longer."

"Yes. It's grisly, but… A pattern of spells of stasis and preservation, and leave him where he died. As his own memorial. And as a reminder to us that we're mortal. That we can't let our vigilance slip."

Chaz leaned out the window, tossed something. Rider asked, "What are you doing?"

"Throwing pop seeds at Su-Cha. He's down there waiting to see if anybody comes for that Emerald."

Spud snickered. "He's been doing it since you left."

Rider looked outside. There were torches on the uppermost platform of the diving tower. The crowd was noisy and restless. "Almost time to go down. Chaz, I want you, Soup, and Preacher to follow me. This would be a good time for our enemies to express their displeasure with us."

"Right."

"Spud, you stay and back up Greystone and Su-Cha."

"Hey! How come I have to miss out?"

Rider tended not to hear such protests. He stepped into the library, where Greystone was perched on a massive oak throne of a chair. It served as the heart of the web for those who, unlike Rider, were unable to make themselves part of it.

"Greystone. What have we got?"

"She's stopped moving." He tapped the map on the table with a pointer. "One of these tenements."

"Right against the river. Heart of the Protte rookery. Not a good place for a woman alone. Fifty thousand foreign sailors and not a ghost of law."

"But a good place for a foreigner to disappear."

"A most excellent place. We'll go down in the morning."

"Why not tonight?"

"These ceremonies. And we're tired. When we're tired we make mistakes. We'll rest. Odehnal will wait."

Rider moved on through the library. Beyond lay a vast suite of rooms he and his father had used from time to time. There he would find apparel appropriate to the awards ceremony. He told Spud, "We'll refurbish these rooms so we can hole up here comfortably."

"Our lives are going to change, aren't they?"

"They have already. It'll be a long time before we comprehend how much."

XI

There was a band to precede the King, and guards in flashy uniforms with ostrich plumes atop their helmets. In a tradition which antedated the celebration of Jehrke Victorious, the King scattered tiny, specially struck silver coins.

"Helps clear the way," he told Rider, who walked beside him. Citizens scrambled wildly as a dozen coins arced into the crowd.

"Cynical attitude."

"Only a cynic and pessimist will survive wearing the crown."

"Or a stoic?"

"My father was a stoic. A very patient stoic. He got a foot of steel stuck into his gizzard. Philosophy means nothing to a dagger." The King seemed more companionable than earlier. Was that a good sign or bad?

As the procession neared the tower, where the medalists waited, onlookers began to murmur about the Protector's absence. Rider was not universally known. But he was recognized by some. His presence fueled speculation.

Shasesserre was a wild and rowdy city. More so on festival days. Fifteen minutes passed before there was order sufficient for the King to speak. He did so at length, dulling the edge of the crowd. He passed the stage to Rider without explaining his presence. Rider presented the victors' laurels with amusing asides and humorous observations, and no more explanation. He finished swiftly, yielded the rostrum to the organizers of the contests.

"So your assassins turned out specters," Belledon said as they pushed through the crowd. "I wonder if half what you've told me isn't imagination."

"We'll see." During his presentation he had felt a tug at the web, just a tiny vibration. Someone learning that the web had been made sound. The deaths of Emerald and Vlazos had not ended the game.

The attack came as the party passed behind an arm of the Rock and started up the incline to the Citadel gate. The King's guards were feeling safe.

A horde of waterfront villains poured out of the dark cracks in the Rock, howling in a dozen languages. Odehnal seemed to have cleared the rookeries. In an instant the guards were all locked in struggle. More thugs swept toward Rider and the King.

Rider's men charged into the fray, falling on the villains from behind.

Rider dipped into pockets, spoke words of power

rapidly. He scattered a handful of small black marbles. Smoke and stench boiled out of them. He shoved the King toward the densest smoke, called his men to join him.

A scarfaced rogue plunged toward him, cutlass reaching. He turned inside the thrust, seized his assailant's wrist. The man shrieked as bones broke. Rider caught the dropped weapon and threw himself between another attacker and Belledon. He used the sword with a skill that would have embarrassed Shasesserre's most famous duelists.

The smoke caused confusion and bought time, but not enough. The evening breeze off the Golden Crescent dispersed it all too soon, and the scene it betrayed was not one to inspire hope.

Most of the King's guards had been slain. A score of attackers remained upright. They began to close in.

Rider became aware of a great warp in the web. Someone had cast a powerful spell. He stood at its center. Everyone and everything within fifty paces was invisible to outside eyes.

No help would come, for no one could see this disaster.

He dipped a hand into a pocket, freed the thing he had loosed at the Vlazos mansion.

His men joined him, the King, and two surviving guards, everyone getting their backs together.

The demon raged. And still the villains came on. What had they been promised?

There was a violent twist in the web. Rider's demon shrieked, dropped a mangled victim, began to spin head over heels. And to shrink. In seconds it dwindled to a point, which vanished with a loud *pop!*

But before it went the monster did, momentarily, frighten the attackers into backing off. Rider turned his attention to the spell that masked the fray.

The attackers again moved in. The area was carpeted with soldiers and assassins. Chaz growled, "These guys must be getting paid gold by the boatload." None were the sort who threw themselves on swords for causes.

The clangor resumed. A guard went down. A blow staggered the King himself. Chaz collapsed, struck on the head. Rider fended blows... He ripped the fabric of the invisibility spell.

Not three seconds later there was a wild bray of trumpets from the Citadel. The garrison was alert already, concerned because the monarch had not yet appeared.

Soldiers poured from the Citadel. The villains saw their deaths upon them. No reward was worth the mercy they could expect if they were captured. They fled.

Groggy, Chaz caught one by the heel and piled onto him.

The very sky seemed to shriek in frustration.

Rider was ready when the deadly sorcery fell. So swift and sure was his response, none of his companions realized they came within seconds of death by melting.

Rider asked the King, "Now will you concede the possibility Shasesserre may be in danger?" But he paid little attention to the response.

That attack had not come from Kralj Odehnal. Of that he was sure. It did not have the dwarf's stamp. Nor did Rider believe Odehnal to be that powerful, nor possessed of so mighty an arrogance.

As he helped Chaz with his prisoner, he told his

men, "This is even bigger than we suspected. And there are more players in the game than we thought."

XII

Rider wakened with the sun. His body ached from the previous day's exertions and bruises, yet he was eager to be at his new vocation. He leapt out of bed, began doing calisthenics.

Su-Cha stuck his head in the doorway. "Up already?" Su-Cha was always up. Imps did not sleep often.

"The juices are flowing, little friend."

"Shall I waken the others?"

"No need. They deserve their rest. How is the prisoner?"

"Unhappy. And as full of blessed ignorance as ought to elevate him direct to nirvana. Someone put sixty pounds of gold on your head. The King's, too. Chaz is going to wilt when he hears his noggin is worth only five."

"What I expected. What of the web?"

"Nothing shaking. His nibs ain't moved."

Rider abandoned his exertions, though customarily he devoted an hour to exercise. "I'll bathe quickly. Two chores to be done. Take your pick. Cook breakfast or fetch shantor's robes for the whole crowd."

"And if I choose cooking?"

"I'll boot you downstairs."

"What I thought." Having little need to consume food, Su-Cha had no need to learn cookery. His occasional efforts verged on the poisonous. "Enough for everybody?"

"Yes. It'll take the whole crew to corner a rat like

Odehnal."

"Remember the old saw."

"I do. I don't expect he'll be taken easily."

Someone in one of the sleeping rooms grumbled about all the racket. Moments later Spud toddled past, headed for the kitchen. He banged around enough to waken everyone else. When Su-Cha returned with the shantor disguises he found the whole crowd tripping over one another while cooking and eating.

The donning of disguises took place not far from the suspect tenements. The weeping sickness was common in the slums, and the terror of the riverbanks. It was a slow and gruesome killer, and one challenge Jehrke had not been able to meet. Rider's men would not stand out unless they made it appear there were too many shantors in one area. People would stay out of their way. Though Jehrke had proven the weeping sickness not to be communicable like measles or the pox, no one believed him.

"Take your time getting into position," Rider told the others. "Don't attract attention. I'll touch you through the web when I'm ready." He sent them off in pairs, ringing their warning bells.

He let a half hour pass. He spent that time touching the neighborhood through the web. There was a disconcerting quiet about it, as though people had sensed Odehnal's presence and knew it augured explosion and terror.

Odehnal was not difficult to locate, this close. The woman Caracené made an outstanding marker. From her Rider caught hints of turmoil, from the dwarf a glowing calm.

There were others in the place. At least four more men, none of whom Rider gave any special attention. They would be the dwarf's hirelings.

He tugged that part of the web which allowed him to touch his associates. *I am going in now,* he sent. *Be alert.*

He moved into the filthy street, stooped, tinkling his shantor's bell. Through a gap between drunkenly leaning tenements he glimpsed the brown dirtiness of the river. Here the old wooden buildings stood with their tails over the water, supported by pilings rising from the bottom mud. These places were always collapsing into the flood, drowning their occupants, and being rebuilt as slovenly as before.

The suspect structure was identical to its neighbors. Rider tinkled from door to door, pausing before each as if begging. When he reached his destination, though, he flicked a finger. A soft click sounded behind the door, a bolt snapping open. There was no guard.

He stepped inside. Behind him one of his men rang his bell.

The darkness within was asphalt thick. He drew a gemlike crystal from a pocket, whispered to it. It began to glow, no more brilliant than a lightning bug. He did not go on till his eyes adjusted.

Odehnal was too confident, Rider thought. No guard, no spell to alert him to intruders. As a soldier Rider had learned that one must always expect the worst in enemy territory.

Eyes adapted, he touched his men again. *I am going upstairs now.* Odehnal was above somewhere. Caracené and the others were in the rear, also upstairs.

Odehnal was not as lax as first glance suggested.

Two thirds of the way up, Rider froze. Something was wrong. He allowed his senses free rein, not moving a muscle. His attention focused upon a stairstep a couple above that where his feet rested.

Even knowing where to look it was a moment before he spied the black thread stretched taut an inch above the worn and grimy tread.

Tricky, setting the trap for a point where an intruder would begin worrying more about what lay ahead. He examined the steps above with even more care. *He* would have set a back-up.

There it was. A step set to trigger an alarm when weight fell upon it.

He stepped over both carefully.

The stair ended on a balcony which ran athwart the building and L-ed to his right. Several doors along the back leaked light beneath them. But Odehnal waited out along the L.

He paused to scatter pop seeds at the elbow of the L, then moved to Odehnal's door. He listened, sensed. The dwarf seemed to be sleeping.

He examined the doorknob minutely. The crystal's light revealed no trap.

Below, he heard the slightest breath of sound. Sunlight poured inside. He saw a shape the size of Chaz slip inside, followed by one of Su-Cha's slightness. He frowned. It was too soon for them to come.

Move quickly!

He turned the doorknob, passed through the doorway swiftly…and stopped, startled, awed.

The room was as opulent as an eastern potentate's private quarters. Odehnal lounged upon huge down-stuffed pillows, face asmile and dreamy. Burnt opium embittered the air.

Quickly, now! Before Chaz or Su-Cha called attention to their presence.

He cast a small spell which sealed Odehnal's lips. He used a modified form of the same spell to join the dwarf's ankles, then his wrists, and even his fingers one to another.

Odehnal stirred once, but only to make himself more comfortable.

A gong hammered in the rear of the house.

Rider hurtled out of the room, into intense light. Chaz stood upon the trap step, a dumb look on his face.

Two men charged out of rear rooms, weapons in hand. Su-Cha materialized between one's legs. He pitched off the balcony with a shriek. The other saw Rider, whirled, charged into the room where Rider knew Caracené and another man to be.

Rider followed, pop seeds exploding beneath his feet. He hurled a shoulder at the door. It burst inward. Chaz breathed down his neck as he entered a room outshining Odehnal's. A thrown knife ripped between them.

In the rear of the room, in shadow, Caracené stood with hands at mouth, looking down. The man who had preceded Rider slammed her out of the way, dropped like a badger plopping into its hole. Caracené scrambled...

Then Chaz had hold of her, and Rider was staring down at a man thrashing through brown water, chasing a boat which meant to waste no time on him.

Rider's gaze fixed on the man in the boat, a lean, powerful oriental with astonishing green eyes. "Shy key, Vlazos said," he murmured. "Shai Khe." One hand came from a pocket clutching a phial. He hurled it.

The man in the boat dropped his oars, raised hands, loosed a warding spell. The phial plopped into the river.

The man saved himself from the misery in that fluid, but lost his oars. He drifted at the mercy of the current.

Rider heard shouts. Soup and Greystone. They had spotted the fugitive. Someone threw a line to the man abandoned.

The oriental's long fingers began weaving sparks. Rider snapped, "Out of here, Chaz. Take the woman. Su-Cha. Get Odehnal." His tone brooked neither questions nor argument.

He drew on the web, began binding it around the sorcerer. Chaz and Su-Cha pounded away.

Too late Rider realized what the oriental was doing. Not attacking him directly at all.

A piling snapped like a twig. The house lurched. Another piling went. The house began to shift, to groan, to tilt toward the river.

Rider did not hesitate. He dropped through the hole, hit the water feet first. He drove himself deep with one powerful stroke, then swam with the current. His strokes were strong and practiced.

The water screamed with the sound of the building collapsing. The scream grew to a roar. But no building comes down in seconds.

When Rider surfaced he was beyond danger of the collapse. Indeed, the structure's main mass smashed into the river as he came up. It raised a wave that lifted him five feet. From the wave's crest he looked at the man in the boat.

The sorcerer's face betrayed frustration. His fingers began weaving again. But the wave caught the boat and toppled him into its bottom. When he recovered Rider had made the riverbank. The oriental wasted no time on an enemy in a position to best him. His boat flew away as though upon a lightning current.

Rider clambered between houses, to the street, where he settled on a stoop to drain his boots.

Chaz settled down beside him, Caracené held almost negligently in one arm. "Who was *that* guy?"

"Shai Khe," Rider replied. "I should have thought of him when Vlazos tried to tell me. He said Shai Khe and I heard shy key."

"That's his name," Chaz said. "But it don't tell me nothing about him." They watched Su-Cha drag Odehnal their way. The dwarf remained imprisoned in his opium dream.

"I know only one thing more," Rider said.

"Uhm?"

"My father was afraid of him."

Chaz looked startled.

"Yes. He wouldn't talk about it. Shai Khe is some great terror in the east. He commands an empire more vast than Shasesserre's. But that does not satisfy him. He wants it all."

Wreckage from the collapsed building drifted away. Rider's men assembled. Neighbors came to watch from a distance safe from shantors.

"More prisoners," Greystone said. The man who had jumped into the river was trying to talk Soup and Spud into turning him loose.

Rider caught his eye. "You're luckier than your

friends." He indicated the wreckage. Two men were in it somewhere. To his own men, he said, "We've done what we can do here. Take these people to the Citadel. We'll question them later. Spud, Su-Cha, Preacher, come with me."

"Where we headed?" Su-Cha asked.

"Airship yards. Before we left the Citadel I sent word for a ship to be readied. We'll use it to hunt Shai Khe. Particularly if he runs to his own ship."

Shai Khe, not Kralj Odehnal, had killed Vlazos and escaped in an unlicensed airship.

Chaz stepped close as Rider was about to leave. He whispered, "What about the girl?"

"Treat her the way she wants you to treat her. If she doesn't suspect she's marked for the web, arrange it so she can escape again. She could lead us again."

"Right. Will do."

Rider and those he had chosen hurried a quarter mile, to where a pair of chariots waited. They shed their shantor's robes as they went.

XIII

Rider's ship was ready. It was a light vessel, capable of carrying just a ton of crew and freight, designed for speed. Rider and Spud went to the control array. There were great magicks involved in the airship's propulsion, but much of its control was mechanical. Spud had helped refine the system.

"Ready to cast off," Rider called to the ground. "Dump ballast, Omar." Rider was the only one of the group to use Spud's proper name. And he forgot much of the time.

Spud tripped levers. The ship began tugging at its restraining lines. "Cast off!" Rider shouted.

The ship lurched upward. Rider murmured to the demonic body, spellbound and beguiled, which constituted its motive force. The airship turned toward the river, began to slide forward like a fish through water.

Aft, Su-Cha and Preacher hastened to take in the mooring lines.

"He was headed Henchelside when last I saw him," Rider said. "And downriver. We'll start looking where Deer Creek Drain runs into the river."

"Keep an eye out for his airship, too," Spud said, making an adjustment to levers which controlled flaps on the ship's sharklike fins. "Be hard to hide something that big."

Rider nodded.

The airship's balance shifted as Preacher and Su-Cha came forward. Spud adjusted with the fins. "Any sign of him?" Su-Cha asked.

"Too soon to tell," Rider replied. The river along Henchelside was crowded with the boats of fisherfolk. Rider directed the demon to follow the shoreline south toward the Golden Crescent. "Take us lower, Omar. I want to see their faces."

There was no tension in the web. Shai Khe was not using his power.

The fisherfolk all looked up as the airship passed over. Rarely did one drop so low.

In time the riverbank curved away westward. The land grew marshy and wild. "Not going to find him this way," Spud said.

"We'll return a ways inland, looking for somewhere

where he might have put his ship down," Rider said. So they ran inland again, as far as that part of the city on Henchelside opposite the Protte rookery. Still they found nothing.

Rider persisted till nightfall made continued search pointless.

"You could turn a hand with this one," Soup complained to Chaz, as they faced the stair to the laboratory. Soup was carrying Odehnal.

"I could. But I like the one I've got just fine." He had Caracené over one shoulder. She was thoroughly bound despite Rider's admonition to treat her well. She wriggled, and squeaked behind her gag. Chaz just grinned at his companions.

Greystone prodded his man with the tip of a sheathed dagger. That fellow never quit protesting his innocence of anything and everything.

At the laboratory door Greystone said, "Somebody tried to get in while we were out." Evidence of attempted entry was obvious. The effort had been a failure, though.

Chaz said, "Vlazos' friends, no doubt."

Greystone popped a signet ring into a small hole in the wall some feet from the doorway. Each of Rider's men wore identical rings. The door responded with a down-scale, musical whine. "Should have done something like this a long time ago."

Soup countered, "When the old man was running things nobody had the guts to try getting in. It'll be that way again when they get used to Rider."

"Let's hope."

One small lumber room had been converted to a

cell for the prisoner already on hand. Odehnal and the other man joined him. "Have you some dinner in a few minutes," Soup told them. "Except you, Odehnal. You'll have to wait on Rider."

The dwarf's eyes smoldered.

Chaz released Caracené in another room. He told her, "Couldn't give you special treatment in front of the dwarf. Sorry."

She did not answer. There was an odd, measuring look in her eyes. She watched him closely still when she sat down to eat with the three men.

"Shai Khe," Greystone said. "An ill name out east. One that strikes terror everywhere. I wouldn't have thought his interest in Shasesserre to be so intense as to bring him here personally." He glanced at Caracené.

She said, "Shasesserre is all that stands between Shai Khe and creation of the greatest empire the world has known."

"He the one gave you to Odehnal?" Chaz asked.

"Yes."

"What can you tell us about him?" Greystone asked.

"Nothing. While he lives, nothing."

"Me, I lost something somewhere, beautiful lady," Chaz said.

"I am his slave." She said that as though it explained all. In her native land, perhaps it did.

"Who?" Chaz insisted. "Odehnal or Shai Khe?"

Caracené bowed her head. Softly, she replied, "Shai Khe."

"Why? You're in Shasesserre."

"There are no slaves in Shasesserre?"

Chaz had to think his way around the side of that.

"He is an enemy of the state. As such he has no rights. You have been freed. We could get you manumission papers by tomorrow."

She looked at him with eyes in which tenderness warred with exasperation. "Paper has no meaning while Shai Khe lives."

Gallantly, Chaz offered, "I'll kick his head in, then. Just tell me where he is."

"I cannot betray him. He is my master."

Soup snickered. Even Greystone smirked.

"I give up," the northerner said. He began muttering about "Women!" under his breath. He cleared his plate and cutlery away, then prepared a tray for the prisoners.

During the afternoon and evening he made every opportunity for Caracené to escape. She did not seize her chance.

Rider reached the laboratory quite late. He examined the prisoners while the others prepared themselves a supper. "Any message from the King?" he asked.

"Nary a word," Chaz replied. "Nothing from anybody."

"I suppose that means he's decided to accept me as Protector—to the extent that he'll ignore me. Till he wants something."

"That's what most of them did with your father. How long you reckon Belledon will last?" Few Shasesserren kings fulfilled normal lifespans. Some years there were three or four self-coronations. Jehrke had held the opinion that the City was its empire's worst enemy. The Protector had provided more stability and continuity than the crown.

"He could be a good one. If he stays alive. Suppose we skip the hired hands and deal with Odehnal directly?"

"A truth-drawing?"

"Get it ready. I'll eat first."

Odehnal's eyes were wild. He was hopelessly caught, for the first time ever at another's mercy. Judging his captors by himself, he was frantic.

"Ought to be interesting," Chaz said, closing the lumber room door. Softly, "The girl wouldn't run."

"I noticed. We'll find him another way."

After eating they brought a more composed Odehnal into the library and strapped him into a chair the twin to that Greystone had used to monitor the web. Rider exercised the utmost caution while unbinding the spells which restrained the dwarf. Odehnal was dangerous still.

"Bit backwards from the way you're used to?" Rider asked. "You willing to tell me what I want to know?" Fear still lurked behind the dwarf's eyes. "Got in over your head when you joined up with Shai Khe, didn't you?"

Odehnal betrayed a flicker of surprise.

"Oh, yeah," Chaz said. "We know about your friend and his pirate airship."

"That being the case, you have no need to question me," Odehnal concluded with a snarl.

"Where is he?" Rider asked.

Silence.

"Do you consider yourself more valuable than Vlazos? He killed Vlazos."

Again Odehnal betrayed a moment's surprise. Vlazos, Rider believed, had been the foot in the Shasesserren door, the lone contact between outsiders and conspirators.

"Let's get on with the truth-drawing, Rider," Su-Cha chirruped. "I love it when they squeal." His cherubic face darkened. "And this one has abused so many of my kind. Let me have him when you're done."

Kralj Odehnal was not to be manipulated by psychological maneuvers. He was old and tough and tempered, and knew all the games interrogators played. He believed he had invented some himself.

Rider shrugged. "Since we have no choice, then."

Greystone placed a contraption on a stand in front of the dwarf. Odehnal looked puzzled. "Spud's special design," Greystone said. "More efficient than candles and mirrors."

Odehnal drew a deep breath…

Chaz stepped behind him, clapped a hand over his mouth. The hand held a wad of cotton impregnated with a fluid of Rider's devising. In moments Kralj Odehnal wore a drugged smile. His head lolled to one side.

Su-Cha stuck him with a hot pin. "Just to make sure he isn't faking."

Rider said nothing, though he knew the Odehnal who was a legend among assassins had self-control sufficient not to start at a pin's prick. "Start it."

Greystone cranked a handle, opened a tiny door. Light flickered upon Odehnal's face. Greystone made a few adjustments.

This was a truth-drawing much less unpleasant than the traditional, which combined a bit of witchcraft with subtle torture. "Waken him," Rider said.

Chaz buried Odehnal's face in cotton moistened

with ammonia. The dwarf sputtered and spat and wakened. His eyes met the light and glazed.

Rider asked several hundred questions, each phrased so a yes or no answer would suffice. Greystone recorded questions and answers and kept his notesheets positioned so Rider could refer to them. The others stayed back, conferring in whispers. Occasionally Soup would dart forward with a note suggesting a question.

The picture that shaped was not one to gladden men devoted to Shasesserre's welfare.

For several years Shai Khe had been recruiting among the sorcerers of the world. Those who refused to make common cause, under his command, he crushed. Those who joined him he gave gifts like Caracené, and powers torn away from those who would not serve him. Now he felt strong enough to test Shasesserre and its Protector.

Rider worked with especial care when he began drawing the names of those Shai Khe had recruited. Yes and no answers were not possible.

Some names amazed him. Some chilled him. Some left him blank, for they were names unknown to him. Those he did know were widely scattered, proving the eastern master had a far reach indeed.

He had drawn just over a dozen names when Odehnal suddenly bucked against his restraints, made squealing noises, and began foaming at the mouth.

"What's wrong with him?" Greystone demanded.

"I don't know… He's dying. Somebody get the medical kit."

Blood flecked the foam on Odehnal's chin.

Rider brushed the hypnotic engine aside, laid hands on the dwarf's heaving chest. He felt the inner wrongness instantly. "Poison!"

"What kind?" Soup demanded, yanking a battery of antidotes out of the medical kit.

"Can't tell. Something different. . . Complex."

Odehnal's eyes opened. Hatred and the knowledge of his own murder filled them. "Polybos House," he croaked. "The Devil's Eyes." His eyes rolled up. He began to shudder violently.

"Rider!" Chaz shouted from the laboratory. "There's something out here."

Rider ripped away from Odehnal, rushed into the darkened laboratory. Chaz was at the window. "Where?"

"Down there now."

Rider leaned out. A shadow clung to the face of the tower, seventy feet below. Points that might have been eyes blinked. A limb of shadow moved. Rider whipped back, into the laboratory an instant before something *tick!*ed against the window frame. "Light," he said. "Get lamps in here." And, "We have to get that pane replaced." He moved to the library door behind Chaz, blocked that against the rush of his men.

"Whatever it was, it shot something at me. It ricocheted off the window frame into the laboratory. Watch where you step. Find it." He took an oil lamp from Preacher, cautiously returned to the window. He leaned out and dropped the lamp.

Down it plunged to smash on the foot of the Rock. He caught one glimpse of something scuttling into darkness.

"What was it? A demon?" Chaz asked.

"No. It was mortal. There was no strain on the web. But exactly what manner of mortal I don't know."

"Here," Soup called.

Rider joined him, looked where he pointed. "A dart. Get tongs. Handle it with care. Let's see if we can't find another around Odehnal."

"This Shai Khe is some nice fellow," Chaz observed. "Kills anybody... Caracené. Where did that woman get to?"

"I think Odehnal getting got, got her moving," Greystone said. He indicated the exit door. It stood open a crack.

"Su-Cha," Rider said. "You follow her. I'll keep in touch through the web."

"Thought you had her *on* the web," Chaz said.

"Not anymore. She figured she was marked and negated it. Su-Cha."

"Yes sir, boss, sir." The imp dived out the window. This time he did not howl on the way down.

Rider moved back to Kralj Odehnal. In a moment he found the lethal dart. "The bodies pile up. And still we make no progress."

"At least they aren't our bodies," Chaz said. "That thing could have gotten one of us as easily as it got Odehnal."

"A point we were meant to take, I'm sure," Rider observed. "A bit more caution from now on, friends. Omar. I want you to fix that window. Soon."

"What do we do now?" Preacher asked.

"We find a place called Polybos House and something called the Devil's Eyes. We stay in touch with the web. And we wait for something to happen."

In the other room the dead eyes of Jehrke Victorious seemed to gleam with approval.

XIV

Su-Cha returned soon after daybreak. He wore a chagrined look. "She shook me in the Protte rookery. I figured she'd cross to Henchelside, so I staked out King's Ferry. She never showed."

Soup snickered. Spud said, "We'll hear from her again. How can she resist that great chunk of beef?" He indicated Chaz, snoring in a chair.

Rider returned from setting Preacher and Greystone to searching land titles for a place called Polybos House. "Soup, you and Omar head down to the Golden Crescent. Look at ships recently in from the east. Find ships that carried unusual cargoes or passengers."

"Why?" Soup asked.

"Shai Khe's airship is a small one. He may have brought more men and equipment than it could have carried. He strikes me as careful and methodical. He would not have come unprepared for a difficult campaign."

Soup and Spud departed. They returned that evening with nothing to report. Preacher and Greystone had no luck either. Greystone said, "If a Polybos House exists it has to be outside the Wall." By that he meant outside the legal corporate limits. The city wall proper lay well inside those, and had been in decay for a century.

"Try again tomorrow," Rider said.

"What're you doing?" Preacher asked.

"Trying to analyze the poison on these darts. It's eluded me so far. Looks like something drawn from an insect, though."

Spud said, "The jungles of Maijan fester with poisonous bugs. And lizards and snakes and bats."

"I'll remember that next time I'm in the far east," Chaz grumbled. He was in a sour mood. He had spent the day washing alembics and retorts under the dead, cold eyes of Jehrke.

"Patience, friend," Rider chided. "Our turn will come."

"Soon, I hope." Chaz tested the window Spud had installed, for the hundredth time. "My nerves are getting me."

Soon did not come for four days.

It began with Soup and Spud. They had, at last, found a vessel whose origins and crew were suspect. After watching the ship, and noting the presence of men of both Emerald's and Shai Khe's races, they decided to contact Rider.

But their persistent presence over several days had betrayed them.

The attack was sudden and bold, initiated by a seaman who stepped into their path and shouted, "At last my brother's daughter's honor will be avenged!" Another half dozen seamen joined him, a wild, scruffy gang of cutthroats.

Spud and Soup were not fooled. The easterner pointed a finger, declared, "You have the wrong men, friend."

The sailor collapsed.

Spud pointed at another man. He went down, too.

Blades came out. A howl went up. More sailors materialized.

Soup, meantime, dipped a hand into his pocket and crushed a crystal. That sent a screaming shock through the web. Then he activated an amulet which Rider could track. Then he scattered fistfuls of what looked like gold coins.

Attackers and onlookers alike dived for the money.

Spud dropped another two men with his pointed finger, ducked inside a clumsy cutlass, buried a fist in a fat belly.

Soup's coins started an independent brawl. They exploded in the hands or pockets of those who had seized them.

Spud pushed away from the man he had punched. "Let's get out of here!" he yelled.

In the confusion that was not difficult. But...

Soup laughed. "The idiots! Hoist by their own greed!"

"Oh-oh," Spud said.

"Yeah."

They had slipped into a breezeway to make their getaway. Their path, suddenly, was blocked by men of Emerald's ilk.

Retreat, too, vanished.

Tough-looking orientals had appeared behind them.

"The coin trick won't work this time."

"I didn't reload my spring gun."

"Been nice knowing you. Take it out on the gnarly guys?"

"Let's get them."

Preacher and Greystone had been butting their heads against a stone wall. There was no Polybos House within fifty miles of Shasesserre, at least on record. They were with Rider, plotting a new strategy, when the web relayed Soup's trouble cry.

"Ask around the merchants' taverns," Rider said, and loped out. A minute later he passed through the Citadel gate in a racing chariot, sounding a warning trumpet. Though the way was longer, he took the Via Triumpha, which by law was closed to wheeled vehicles. Because there was no commerce there, few pedestrians were about.

The Via's prime function was as a processional for military holidays, and for the celebration of major victories.

Rider swung off the Via Triumpha a quarter mile from where his men had found trouble. During his mad flight he had acquired an escort of City Guards, who had recognized him and were carrying warning ahead. They made passage through the waterfront district much easier.

So quick was Rider to reach the scene that the crowd had not yet dispersed. A dozen people lay unconscious, not yet carried off by comrades. "Collect these and deliver them to the Citadel," Rider told his escort. He left his chariot and set off after the moving disturbance the web noted as the location of his men.

He found the back-up ambush. There were signs of a vigorous fight, and spilled blood. Had Soup and Spud been slain, their bodies carried off with those of their enemies?

His heart sank. Shai Khe was a relentless and merciless opponent.

He allowed his wizard's senses to extend. This was a good time and place to jump someone tracking the missing men.

They were there, just ahead in the breezeway, hidden beneath trash and inside shadows. There were eight of them. They had several mystical devices that would have been potent had they taken Rider unaware. They were growing impatient.

Rider produced a deck of plaques the size of tarot cards. He shuffled out the one he wanted. It portrayed a man asleep, dreaming hideous devils. The devils were about to seize and drag him through a fiery gap in a background wall. There were graven words around the plaque's margin. Rider read them aloud.

As he spoke each word, it disappeared. After he spoke the last, the picture itself faded. The plaque crumbled into dust which dribbled between his fingers.

Rider went back and told the City Guards they could collect another eight customers in the breezeway. Then he set out after the receding disturbance marking the location of his men.

He loped to the waterfront, where he immediately identified both the vessel they had unmasked and the outbound fishing smack carrying them. The ship reeked of old sorceries forgotten by all but their victims.

Rider raced back to his chariot, pounded through the streets to the airship yards, where, in accordance with standing instructions, his airships were ready for immediate flight. He selected the fast vessel he had used before.

Liftoff was hectic, as he had to cover the places of crewmen not present, but once he was aloft he had no trouble. He reached through the web, touched Chaz and Preacher, told them he wanted everyone atop their tower of the Citadel. He tried to reach Soup and Spud, but a grey null intervened. They might be unconscious. Or worse.

Chaz and Su-Cha were in the parapet when Rider halted the airship above the Citadel. Both carried packs. Rider hastened to the gondola door, dropped a rope ladder. As Chaz and Su-Cha scrambled up, Greystone and Preacher appeared.

"What's up?" Chaz demanded as he clambered aboard.

"The game is afoot. They snatched Spud and Soup. What are the packs?"

"Some odds and ends we threw together. Just in case."

"The laboratory secure?"

Su-Cha chuckled. "And then some."

XV

Chaz repeated the news for Preacher and Greystone. Rider ordered the ship demon to proceed toward the Golden Crescent at speed, for the fishing boat was near the limit of the web. He had to get the vessel in sight first or lose it among a hundred others.

"I think I've been outmaneuvered," he said.

"How's that?" Chaz asked.

"The boat is leaving the web. To follow we'll have to keep it in sight. Which means they'll be able to see us, too."

"How about an invisibility spell?"

"Wouldn't hide something this big."

"What about an angel?" Su-Cha asked. Already he had shed his shirt and sprouted wings.

Rider understood immediately. "An albatross or eagle would be less flashy."

"Dig out some of those mirrors and flares," Su-Cha

told Chaz. Already his head was avian.

"A shape to go with his brain," Chaz said, ransacking the packs. He produced signal mirrors and four small flares, which he placed in a pouch the imp grew among his ventral feathers. Su-Cha retained rudimentary hands beneath his wings.

Rider spread a maritime chart. "The ship is here, now, and headed so. If there are others around, watch the one that is in a hurry. They're making all the speed they can."

Su-Cha squawked and plunged through a hatch Preacher opened. In a moment he was headed out over the strait on long white wings.

Greystone looked over Rider's shoulder. "They headed for the Hurm Islands?"

"Maybe. They could shift course once they're sure they're clear of the web."

"How soon?"

"I've lost them already."

"Signal from Su-Cha," Chaz said. "He has them."

Rider peered out the window. Far away, a mirror flashed.

"Keeping their heading," Chaz read.

"Tell him not to get too close," Rider replied. "What do you know about the Hurm Islands, Greystone?"

"Not much to know. Uninhabited and considered uninhabitable. Except for the biggest, Radhorn Island, they're little more than marshy places off the mouth of the Claytyne River." The Claytyne emptied into the Bridge of the World from its southern, Saverne side. "Long ago, before the seas were ours alone, there were naval fortifications on Radhorn. Earlier still, pirates nested there, lying in wait for ships headed west."

Rider nodded. "And these days it's suspected of being a hideout for smugglers. The ruins of the fortifications would provide a good hiding place for a pirate airship."

"But Odehnal said Polybos House," Preacher protested.

"Let's forget that for the moment. Chaz. Can you make out Su-Cha?"

"Only when he flashes an all right."

"Maybe we ought to call for an all-out raid," Preacher said. "Half a dozen airships and a company of air marines. Could be anything waiting out there."

"If it becomes necessary." Rider spoke to the propulsive demon. The ship surged forward. "Chaz. We're going down channel and crossing over. Tell Su-Cha." He began shedding altitude.

The airship crossed the Bridge of the World just yards above the waves. It was seen by several merchantmen and fishing vessels, but Su-Cha reported none steering near the Hurm Islands. Rider took the airship up into the southern hills, finally grounded in a side canyon leading down to the Claytyne River.

"Now what?" Chaz asked. He was working his sword with a whetstone.

"We wait for darkness. And for Su-Cha."

Su-Cha arrived first, but not by much. "They stuck Soup and Spud in a basement under the old ruins, then headed back for the north shore."

"They just dumped them?" Chaz asked. "Didn't leave any guards or anything?"

"Oh, there's guards. Fifteen or twenty smugglers and runaway slaves and such, that they paid to watch them."

Chaz said, "Something's wrong here, Rider. Either

it's a trap or we've been snookered into leaving town."

"No trap," Su-Cha said. "I looked the place over good."

"Perhaps Shai Khe has fallen victim to his own arrogance."

"Well, at least we could have followed the fishing boat if the runt hadn't…"

Su-Cha was grinning his biggest grin.

"What instructions were the smugglers given as to the care of our friends?" Rider asked.

"They're to treat them well. Till they hear otherwise. The men from the boat—they were all orientals—paid the smugglers for two weeks."

"And did you do what I suspect you did with your flares?"

"Yep." Su-Cha grinned again.

"And your mirrors?"

"Right up on the masthead. Nobody pays attention to a bird."

"Or a birdbrain," Chaz mumbled.

Rider said, "Let's get flying, then. Soup and Spud are safe for the moment."

"You just going to leave them there?" Chaz asked.

"If we don't mess with them, Shai Khe will think we're off the trail," Su-Cha said.

Rider took the airship back along the reverse of his approach route, but midway across the Bridge of the World he lifted into the normal air lane from Kaizherion. "Take over, Chaz."

He busied himself in the rear of the cabin for several minutes. In time he brought forward a plate of frosted violet glass. He handed this to Su-Cha. The imp held it at eye level, extended, in both hands. "Ready when you are."

Rider spoke one Word of Command. Su-Cha turned rapidly, staring through the glass. "There!"

Rider marked the direction. "Charts, Greystone. Not the direction I expected."

"Thought they would head for the City?" Su-Cha asked.

"Yes."

The boat was bound westward.

Rider examined the chart. "They're hugging the coast. Trying to slip past the patrol in the Narrows. Go down, Chaz. Let's see if we can't raise the guardship."

Finding the Narrows sentinel was simple. The trireme was showing her lights. There were no challengers on Shasesserre's seas.

Rider went down the rope ladder, spoke with the vessel's commander. When he returned, he said, "All set."

Su-Cha squealed maliciously, then spoke the Word of Command that ignited the flares aboard the fishing boat.

The trireme was headed north already, cadence drum pounding. "They'll make it look like a rescue," Rider said. "But then they'll stay on station till they're relieved. Shai Khe will have to do without those men for a while."

"We could use a few for a truth-drawing." Chaz opined.

"The captain will turn them in as suspected smugglers. They'll be available."

"There she goes!" Su-Cha crowed.

A growing fire illuminated the strait.

"Pity we couldn't follow them," Chaz said.

Rider mused, "I don't think they would have led us anywhere. I suspect their function *was* to draw us away." He shrugged. "We'll see. Meantime, Shai Khe is short even more of his resources. Those can't be infinite."

XVI

Rider used the ladder to deposit Chaz and Su-Cha atop the Citadel, then returned the airship to its cradle. It was near dawn when he reached his laboratory. Chaz opened the door grinning.

"Good news?"

"Good and bad," Chaz said. "The good is, we had visitors. They're still here."

"The woman?"

"How did you know?"

"It seemed reasonable. She saw a ring used to open the door. I assume that is how she got inside?"

Chaz nodded. "She used Soup's. The guy used Spud's."

"Guy?"

"Look him over. He wants to play hard-boy. Wouldn't talk to us."

"All right. What's the bad news?"

"Two kinds of it. Somebody let out the prisoners you took this afternoon. People are claiming it was all a mixup and misunderstanding, but a couple City Guards got themselves killed. And Kentan Rubios is dead. The King wants to see you about that."

"He was murdered?"

"Belledon thinks he was. I already talked to the physician. Says he didn't find anything suspicious."

Rider checked to see if there had been disturbances

in the web while he was out of touch. None were evident. Shai Khe was playing a careful game where the web was concerned. Perhaps he had come in contact with it before and been burned by Jehrke.

The library contained two outsiders, each still as a statue. Caracené was one. Her eyes gleamed fear. The other was a well-dressed man, though his clothing was a little flashy. He seemed more resigned than frightened.

"Searched him?" Rider asked.

"Yep. Down to his socks." Chaz indicated ten pounds of razor-sharp cutlery upon the library table. "Regular walking arsenal, this guy."

"I'll release him from the field," Rider said. He ignored Caracené.

Chaz drew his sword.

Rider negated the static spell which held the captives. Caracené staggered. Greystone and Preacher caught her, placed her firmly into a chair. Rider offered a second chair to the other captive. The man seated himself with dignity. He kept his hands carefully in sight.

"A professional," Chaz said.

Rider nodded. Of the man, he asked, "Do I need to indulge in a truth-drawing?"

"You'd be wasting your time. I don't know anything."

"Perhaps. Who gave you the ring you used to gain entry?"

"Sanjek Polybos House."

Rider concealed his astonishment. The others were less successful. The prisoner seemed not to notice.

"Your assignment?" Rider asked.

"Pick up anything he might find interesting."

"That's pretty general. Wasn't he more specific?"

The captive thought a moment. He eyed Greystone, who was setting up for a truth-drawing, just in case. "He did mention a key to a Treasury lock box. Nothing else specific. I got the impression papers and documents would be of considerable interest."

"Your name?"

The man smiled. "Zantos? Yes. Zantos Leaela."

Rider nodded. In a Saverne side country dialect the name meant approximately Stranger Dark As Night. More colloquially, Shadowman. In a way, what Rider had expected from his first glimpse of the man. "Put him in the lumber room."

"You made sense out of that?" Chaz asked, once the prisoner was out of the way.

"Yes. He's one of the King's Shadows."

"The secret agents who watch for sedition? But…"

"Sanjek Polybos House," Rider said. "We have been mistaken again. We were looking for a place, a building, when we should have been looking for a person." He took Vlazos' key from his pocket. "A person very high up, who is part of the conspiracy." Sanjek, as a title, ranked with legate, legionary commander, or general. Rumor said five men of sanjek rank controlled the King's Shadows. One ranked the other four and reported directly to King Belledon. Of the others, one was responsible for the City, another for the Home Territories. The other two oversaw the eastern and western provinces of the empire.

"Obviously, Shai Khe has found ways around Vlazos' death."

Rider faced Caracené. "And what was your mission?"

"I was not sent. I came to warn Chaz…"

"Been singing us the same song," Su-Cha said. "As if anybody is fool enough to believe that even the big thug's own mother would give him warning…"

The barbarian snagged Su-Cha from behind. His meaty hands surrounded the imp's neck. He wore several silver rings. Su-Cha could not escape. Chaz lifted him chest high. "Should we stew him or fry him?"

"Warn Chaz about what?" Rider asked.

Caracené would say no more.

"Chaz?"

"The way I get it, Kentan Rubios expected an attempt on his life." He beamed at Caracené. Su-Cha kicked and squeaked, to no avail. "He talked about asking us to help. One of the conspirators heard. When Shai Khe found out, he sent men to intercept any messengers coming from Rubios."

"Did a message come?"

"No."

"Interesting. But you didn't explain why Caracené is here."

"Rubios *was* supposed to be killed. She was afraid I might try to stop it and get myself hurt."

Su-Cha unleashed a wild, braying, peacock peal of derisive laughter. Chaz cut it off by squeezing his throat.

"So. Independent confirmation of Belledon's suspicions."

"You going to see him?"

"Soon. Yes. He may know more than I thought. And I should let him know what we've found out."

"What about our spy?"

"We'll keep him till we track down Polybos House.

But we'll let him go eventually. He hasn't done any evil." Rider fingered the Vlazos key. That bore immediate investigation if someone wanted it recovered. "I'd best get to it."

At the door, Chaz whispered, "What about the woman?" He now carried Su-Cha in one hand, toes dragging, like a child dragging a doll.

"Hold on to her. If she's told the truth, she's put herself in danger."

XVII

"Well," Soup said as Spud sat up, clutching his head. "We're alive. For now."

"Where are we?" Spud asked. And, "What did they give us? I've never had a hangover like this."

"I don't know. To both. With me it's my stomach."

"They dragged us onto a ship. I remember that."

"This is no ship." Darkness surrounded them. So did the odors of damp earth and rot. "You tied up?"

"Yeah. Are you?"

"Yes. But I think I can get loose."

A bright square of light materialized overhead, nearly blinding them. Vague dark shapes looked down. "You guys awake?"

Spud saw no need to pretend otherwise. "Yeah."

"Good. Ready to eat?"

"How the hell are we going to eat tied up like this?"

"I don't know. That's your problem. We just get paid to watch and feed you."

"Where are we?"

"In a hole in the ground." Both men above laughed. One lowered a basket by rope.

"Hurry it up," one jailor said. "I ain't going to sit here all day."

"Hell, let the rope go," the other said.

The line snaked down. The square of light vanished. Soup asked Spud, "What do you make of our new quarters?"

"Only what we know already. It's an old cellar of some kind."

"Those weren't the guys who caught us."

"Hired thugs."

"How do we get out?"

"First let's get untied. Step at a time."

"I'm almost loose… There. Be done in a minute."

It took longer. Soup's fingers were numb. But in ten minutes both men were free. Soup said, "Shall we sample our host's hospitality?"

"Your stomach better? My head is still pounding."

"A little. I'm starved. We must have been out a long time."

They emptied the basket.

They used the rope to measure their prison. It was twenty-one paces by twelve, and in terrible repair. One end wall was partly collapsed. But that was no help.

Spud found human bones. Neither he nor Soup cared to speculate on their significance.

Soup said, "Looks like the only way out is the way we came in."

"Yeah. How high you figure that was?"

"Twelve feet."

"We could reach it if I stood on your shoulders."

"Maybe. If we could find it. If it isn't locked or

something. And if there isn't a guard outside. If I was guarding I'd sit on the lid."

"Best time would be at night, wouldn't it? Real early in the morning night."

Soup asked, "How are you going to know?"

The darkness was dense in that pit. It was a darkness so dense it set the eye to seeing imaginary spooks. But it was not a darkness reserved to them alone. Whenever they were silent for a time, small things rustled. Sometimes it seemed the things were not so small.

"There," Spud said.

"What?"

"Made a lariat out of the rope."

"What good is that?"

"I don't know. Yet. It's a tool. The only one we have. Maybe I could rope the guy and pull him in."

Soup did not think much of that. "Maybe we ought to sit tight."

"You think Rider knows where we are?"

"There's a good chance."

They sat tight a few hours because they had no choice.

Next time a meal came through the hatchway the light was weaker outside. Spud complained, "How about you guys untie us? There's rats down here."

Only one man had come. He laughed. "You don't eat for a few days, those ropes will loosen up." He lowered another basket.

"Keep him talking," Soup whispered.

Spud did his best. Soup examined their prison.

It had been used as a garbage pit. And dump for bodies. He saw fragments of several skeletons. But nothing useful as a tool or weapon.

"Quit your whining," the man above said. "You're alive." And, "I heard you guys was tough. Guess maybe you're not so much after all." He laughed as Spud spat something back.

The easterner demolished the man's claim to a family history.

The light went out.

"I think you made him mad, Spud."

Spud chuckled. "That was the idea. Look up there."

Soup saw a hairline crack of light.

They argued about who would climb onto whose shoulders. The fading of the light caused Soup to give in.

Spud fell off his first two tries. Third time around he caught hold and kept his balance. Soup huffed and muttered. Spud strained and stretched, forced the tips of his fingers through the crack. He ground his teeth, expecting a heel to smash them.

Nothing happened.

He pulled himself up, pushed the cover with his head. "Heavy!" he gasped.

"Hurry!" Soup growled. "You're ruining my shoulders."

Spud heaved again. A corner of the lid rose. Then the whole thing slid aside. He threw an arm over the edge of the hole, anchored himself, looked around. "Nobody up here." A moment later he was out. "The rope!" he said.

It came up. He hoisted Soup. They swung the lid into place.

"Where are we?" Soup asked.

"Someplace near the Bridge. Tell that by the smell."

"Yeah. Looks marshy down there… What's that?"

A whiny, muted, metallic sound came from the north. "Music," Soup said.

"If you say so." Spud coiled his lariat. "Let's take a look."

In a moment they crouched behind a fallen wall, looked at a shabby building which leaked light and sound. A door opened on the far side. Enough light escaped to betray a small ship drawn up on a narrow beach.

"Smugglers," Soup said. "They hired smugglers to watch us."

"What now?"

"Put some distance between us and them. Hole up till dawn. Then head along the coast till we come to a village."

Spud snorted. "We'll see."

"We won't see much for long if we don't start stepping."

The sun had not been up an hour before they knew the awful truth. "An island!" Soup snarled. "We're on an island."

"One of the Hurm Islands, to be exact," Spud said. "Nowhere else fits."

"So we're trapped anyway."

"We'll steal a boat. We're not that far from the Saverne side."

Soup demanded, "How do you expect to do that? It won't be long before they know we're gone and start hunting. We can't grab one of their boats in broad daylight."

"We won't. I'll lower you back down so you can grouch and complain when they come to feed us. I'll pull you out again after dark. Then we'll grab a boat. And have twelve hours' head start."

"Why don't *you* go down in the hole?"

"It's my plan."

Bickering, they headed for their former prison.

XVIII

Rider was thoughtful as he descended to the Treasury chambers.

"Why so quiet?" Su-Cha asked. In the shadows the imp was almost invisible. He gave Rider a start.

"I'd better pay more attention," Rider said. "You could have been one of Shai Khe's gang."

"Right. I could. So what did Belledon say?"

"That Kentan Rubios was the chief of the King's Shadows."

"Aha."

"Aha indeed. Polybos House—a pseudonym, of course— is the only other sanjek in the City."

"Aha again. Where are you headed?"

"To look into Vlazos' safety chest. Afterward, we'll visit Rubios' City house. Belledon said he ordered everything left as it was found."

"What's he going to do about Polybos House?"

"Call him in for a conference and surprise him with a set of chains. We get first crack at him."

"What was that?" They were near the Treasury vault, deep in the living stone of the Rock. The hallways were nests of shadows.

Rider saw nothing, but trusted Su-Cha's senses. He took hold of the web, probed. "Something… The thing that murdered Odehnal. It's gone now. Evidently just spying."

"You'd better be quick. He might have gone for help."

"He probably did." Rider lengthened his stride. "Keep watch."

Two old pensioners guarded the vault. They knew Rider. He had a Treasury secure chest of his own. He gave them a sealed order from Belledon. Half the security of the vault arose from the fact that only the vault attendants themselves could distinguish between the thousands of identical chests.

They argued. Not even the King, they said, could authorize…

Rider waved a hand. They fell silent. "Show me the box," he commanded.

The elder turned, led the way. The other remained on guard, occasionally shaking his head puzzledly. Su-Cha vanished into the shadows outside.

Rider's guide indicated a chest indistinguishable from a hundred others. Rider tried the Vlazos key. The chest opened immediately.

"Ah." Several bound ledgers lay inside the chest, with one packet of letters tied together with a red ribbon. Rider opened a ledger at random.

Names. Dates. Places. Minutes of topics discussed.

"This is what I came for." He took ledgers and letters and headed for the door.

Su-Cha sent warning by tugging at the web.

Rider cast a small spell which set shadows dancing like a madman's dream. Those who lurked outside became disoriented. They called to one another in confusion.

A second spell sent shadows playing over Rider's own body. He entered the chaos in the hallway—and seemed to disappear.

Su-Cha, meantime, shifted form. He grew into something huge and ugly, a nightmare beast with eight-inch fangs and a disposition so foul fire bubbled from his nostrils. He jumped at a man. "Boo!"

Panic added its mad whip to the confusion.

The two old guards came to investigate. Su-Cha frightened them, too. He giggled, then took off after Rider.

"Names, dates, places, and plans," Rider told the others. The contents of Vlazos' chest lay scattered across the library table. "A meticulous man, our Vlazos. He kept records of everything."

"When do we round them up?" Chaz asked.

"We'll let Belledon have the credit for that," Rider said. "We're going to Kentan Rubios' house."

"Let Belledon do it? When you can't trust anyone anymore?"

Rider tapped the ledgers. "He'll have these to go by."

"But they know about them. Else why would a bunch of them have been down at the vault?"

"Maybe we'll see the rats scatter," Su-Cha said. "Rider, you think Belledon will grab Polybos House? Because we still got to figure out about the Devil's Eyes."

"Things are going to get crazy, we'd better see about Spud and Soup, too," Chaz said. "Shai Khe might kill them out of spite."

"I don't think he's the petty sort," Rider said. "Still,

he can't keep a close rein on all his henchmen. We'll go first time things slow down."

Chaz jerked his head to indicate Caracené. "What about her?"

"We can't have her running off, can we? She knows what we know. I'll set the doors and window so they can't be opened from inside or out... What's that?"

"Somebody pounding on the door."

Rider strode into the laboratory. Chaz ducked into the contraption of mirrors. "It's all right," Rider said, after peering through the peeping device. "One of the King's men." He opened the door.

Chaz was determined to trust no one. Likewise, Su-Cha, who had secreted himself behind a rack of glassware. Even Preacher and Greystone, in the library, had drawn weapons.

The King's man did not enter. Breathlessly, he said, "His Majesty has taken the prisoner. But people from the Shadows are clamoring to talk to him. His Majesty suggests you take custody."

Inside his hiding place, Chaz snorted derisively.

Rider replied, "I'll do that. But not right away. Tell him he might reduce the clamor by giving the Shadows an assignment. Chaz. Get me those ledgers."

When Chaz returned with the books, Rider told the messenger, "His Majesty should find these very interesting. They should tell him what to do till I can get to him."

The messenger accepted the load with ill grace, departed.

"You think he's going to be safe, walking around with those?" Chaz asked.

Rider, concentrating, raised a hand that asked for

silence. He wove mystic patterns with his fingers, clapped his hands. "That should do it."

"Do what?"

"Fix him so people won't notice him."

"You made him invisible?"

"That would have been too difficult and too time-consuming. No. He'll just not seem worth paying attention to."

"What now?"

"Now we go see how Kentan Rubios died."

Rider had his associates assemble certain equipment. Five minutes later, they left. Chaz stalled outside the laboratory door. Suddenly, he grinned. "She's not that anxious to stay after all."

Someone was trying to get the door open.

"It's your overpowering charm," Preacher said. "She can't stand to be parted from you."

Chaz looked hurt. "Hey! I maybe got to take that from the runt, here, but from you I don't…"

Su-Cha cackled. "You bring it on yourself."

"We don't have all day," Greystone observed from down the hallway.

They hurried to catch up.

Greystone asked Rider, "How long before Shai Khe hears Polybos House is incommunicado and gets suspicious? He hasn't been reluctant to shed potential embarrassments."

"I've been wondering myself. Especially since the appearance of those men near the vaults." Rider ordered chariots brought for them. "We suffer the disadvantage of all defenders. We don't know where or when the enemy will strike next."

Greystone observed, "A closer study of those ledgers

might yield a few hints."

Chaz snorted. "How?"

"They not only tell who is part of the conspiracy, by omission they tell us who isn't. Among those who aren't named we'll find the men Shai Khe will want to remove."

"True," Rider agreed. "And we'll look at that angle. But more, we need to strike back. We need to get on his tail and stick. To keep him moving. To take away his time to plan murders."

A black wreath decorated the gate to Kentan Rubios' Balajka estate. It was the only outward show of tragedy's having struck. A gateman let them into the grounds. Rider stared around narrowly. "Su-Cha, you and Chaz look for traces left by an uninvited guest. Greystone, Preacher, stay with me."

Su-Cha and Chaz dismounted. Servants moved the chariots aside and began caring for the horses. Su-Cha began walking the base of the estate wall, sniffing. Chaz followed, looking bored, pestering the imp with unpleasant remarks. There was little else he could contribute.

A footman led them to the atrium, where a household servant met them and said, "Doctor Recer has remained with the Lord. I fear he has grown impatient. We all expected you sooner."

"We had hoped to arrive sooner," Rider said, and extended gracious apologies. "Our enemies kept us busy. I'll smooth the doctor's feathers."

The body lay on a couch in a library. The doctor and a woman of the household staff were waiting nearby. After extended apologies and social amenities, Rider said, "Describe the circumstances surrounding the death."

Greystone and Preacher began prowling the book-shelves, the former making little sounds of awe whenever he spotted a tome he especially coveted.

The woman replied, "The Lord had closed himself in here, leaving instructions that he was not to be bothered. At about the tenth hour he cried out. Several of us went to the door, but found it locked. He cried out again. 'Keep away, shadow,' we think he said. When the men broke the lock they found him sprawled on the floor."

Rider was standing before a window, watching Su-Cha and Chaz while he listened. Now he interrupted. "On the floor? I was assured nothing would be disturbed."

Doctor Recer said, "There is no evidence that he died of aught but natural causes. His position was undignified."

Rider interrupted, speaking to the woman. "This window is locked. Was that his custom?"

"Yes, sir. It was. When he was working on something important."

"Yet he shouted at someone or something." Outside, Su-Cha's gestures, as he spoke to Chaz, indicated that he had found the point where something had crossed the wall.

"Rider?" Greystone said. "Look here."

The scholar was kneeling beside the room's one anomaly, an overturned chair. He pointed. A splinter of leg was split loose. Grey-brown hairs were caught there.

Rider squatted, considered, grunted. Then he went to the fireplace, in which no fire had been laid. Soot speckled clean firebrick. To the doctor, he said, "Examine him again. Look for a puncture such as might have been made by a pin." He continued to examine the fireplace. Inside, caught on a brick, he found another hair.

"Well?" Greystone asked.

"I think it was the same thing that killed Odehnal. It must be very agile and fairly intelligent."

Preacher looked up the chimney. "Skinny, too. This is a tight fit."

The doctor loosed a soft explosion of breath.

"You found it?"

"Yes." Recer indicated a tiny purple bruise centered by a pinhead scab on the corpse's hip. "Not that it's especially noteworthy. The man had a history of heart problems."

"Yes." Rider cut off the excuses, turned to the woman. "Is anything missing?"

She shrugged. "We were not permitted to come in here."

In minutes Rider knew her for a well gone dry. Kentan Rubios had been a secretive man.

Su-Cha blew in bubbling with his news. Rider indicated the hairs snagged on the chair leg. "Can you get enough from that to trail the creature?"

Su-Cha snuffled while Chaz made rude remarks.

The imp grinned. "Got it. A close thing, too. Any imp but me couldn't have managed it." He hustled out the door. Chaz grumbled in his wake.

Rider told the doctor, "We're finished. You can remove the body now."

"Don't you want to interview the rest of the staff?"

"That won't be necessary. Tell His Majesty his suspicions were well-founded. That we are on the trail of the killer. Greystone. Preacher. Come."

XIX

Rider overtook Su-Cha a block up the street. The imp looked crestfallen. "It boarded a vehicle here."

Rider was not surprised. "A closed coach, I'm sure. It would have spent some time waiting."

Chaz caught on before Su-Cha did. He guffawed.

Preacher observed, "Horses are as full of offal as the Lord is with mercy, and have no more sense of propriety than a northern barbarian."

Chaz shut up. He glared at Preacher, not quite sure what had happened.

Su-Cha scowled but contained his pride. He sought the trail of the horses.

Greystone, ever attentive to detail, observed, "We're being watched. That man yonder picked us up at the gate."

Chaz glared at the loiterer, who was having trouble looking like part of the landscape. His sort did not belong on the Balajka Hill. "Want me to grab him, Rider?"

"Later, perhaps. Keep an eye on him. And keep another out for somebody watching him. Su-Cha. Can you track the horses or not?"

"Yes." The imp's reply was curt. His expression dared disparaging remarks.

"Head in the right general direction but don't follow them exactly," Rider said.

"Eh? Why?"

"Our nervous friend may be there to see if we can pick up the trail. We don't want him to run off and set up an ambush."

"Let's ambush him," Chaz urged. His blood was up. He was sick of being frustrated. He wanted to smack somebody around.

"We will," Rider said, his thoughts and plans shifting momentarily. "Once we know if he's being watched in his turn."

Chaz chuckled wickedly.

They walked a block past where Su-Cha said the assassin had turned. Rider said, "We'll go this way," and turned the opposite direction. That put them round the corner of a wall, out of view of the man who followed.

Rider reached into the web and drew power, hastily spun images of himself and Su-Cha. He did not have time to weave them well. In ten minutes they would begin floating between steps and leaking light through their bodies.

Rider swarmed up the wall, Su-Cha at his heels. From the wall's top, Rider said, "Lead him along. Work your way back to the chariots. Lose him, then take the way Su-Cha pointed out," all in a rush. The web told him the watcher was nearby.

Tentative footsteps rounded the corner. Rider peeked carefully. The man seemed satisfied he was on the right track.

Rider reached into the web, seeking a watcher of the watcher. He found one quickly. "Another one coming," he breathed.

This man's steps indicated great self-confidence. Rider let him pass, raised his head carefully. A man of

Shai Khe's race. He murmured, "Mark him carefully, Su-Cha. If we lose the horses we can follow him."

"Rider."

Su-Cha's tone said they had trouble. Rider shifted and looked.

A night gardener squatted among moon poppies, milk pot and milking fork in hand, gaping at them. He did not seem inclined to cause a fuss. Maybe he thought he'd caught an inadvertent whiff of pollen.

The oriental tracker's attention was directed in front of himself. Rider cast a small glamor that left the gardener shaking. He would be sure he had breathed pollen.

"He's out of sight," Su-Cha said. "Let's go."

Rider jumped down. Su-Cha floated. They trotted into the street down which the assassin had departed his handiwork. Rider left a small chalk mark at each crossway, to indicate which direction he had gone.

The trail departed the Balajka district and its quiet, almost untenanted streets, dipping into an area occupied by merchants, tending downhill toward the Golden Crescent. The quality of their surroundings deteriorated. The farther they descended, the busier the night became, despite the hour.

Rider slowed the pace. He kept a greater part of his attention in the web, observing his surroundings. Su-Cha he charged with using his preternaturally sharp eyes and nose. In crowds like these it would be hard to spot Shai Khe's confederates. Dawn found them very near the waterfront, in a warehouse district. The assassin had traveled a long way.

XX

Pure good luck attended Spud and Soup. They slipped a boat away unnoticed, caught a brisk breeze, made a landfall not a half mile from a legionary encampment. The prefect of the camp was a friend of Rider and Jehrke. Within an hour they were crossing the Bridge of the World aboard the legion's courier airship. First light was just starting to limn the City when they stepped down into the jungle of the military yards.

Though they were as far from the exit gate as they could get, they grinned at one another and set off jauntily. Spud whistled as he walked.

Minutes later Spud's tune died behind Soup's hand. Both ducked into shadows.

Soft voices approached. They saw men moving quickly, cautiously, probing shadows with shielded lights, arguing.

"Those knobbly guys again," Spud said. "What're they doing *here*?"

"Right now they're looking for a whistler."

Spud reddened. "Let's get them."

"I admire your confidence. Nevertheless, the odds aren't exciting for one of my delicate sensibilities." There were six gnarly men, none of whom were completely alert. They were going through the motions of a search, complaining.

"Let's even them up, then." Spud vanished, moving with feline silence.

Soup sighed. Spud was in one of his moods. He would not give it up till he bashed a few heads. Or got bashed himself. Soup retreated the way he had come. Twenty feet back, he kicked a wooden support away from an airship cradle still under construction. He ducked behind the cradle.

The noise brought the gnarly men his way.

Spud stepped out behind the last and smacked his head with a board. He jumped back into shadow.

Gnarly men chattered at one another. Knives came out. Lights probed shadows diligently.

Soup took his turn crowning a man. When the gnarly men turned to rush him, Spud struck again.

Then Rider's men waded in. Confused, howling, the gnarly men panicked. They fled into striped shadows. The yards resembled a boneyard populated by the skeletons of monsters more vast than any leviathan of the deep. The dawn itself was as bloody as a newly mown army.

Soup and Spud skidded to a halt, dove into cover. The gnarly men had joined a young regiment working around a monster of an air warship from the eastern fleet. Soup sputtered, "They're trying to steal that airship!"

Chaos spread as the fugitives reported.

Spud observed, "Some big payoffs must have been made to let that many men sneak in here." An entire cohort guarded the military yards.

"Couldn't be all of them, though," Soup observed.

"No. Just a few officers and noncoms. A big enough racket ought to get the rest out here."

"What're you going to do? Howl like a mad dog?"

The *how* did present a problem. They had come out of captivity with nothing but their clothing.

"Better think of something fast," Soup said. "They're not going to wait around." The would-be airship thieves were organizing a counterstroke.

Soup found himself talking to empty air.

He found Spud searching the apparel of a fallen gnarly man. "Aha. Here we go. Now something flammable."

Soup thought he got the idea. He also thought it was too dangerous. If the fire got out of hand the whole yard could go. Nevertheless, he collected a pair of dropped lanterns. One still burned. He tuned it up high, whirled like a hammer thrower in the athletic games, arced it toward the gas bladders.

"What are you, crazy?"

Soup glared. What did Spud want? He collected another lantern. "Light this." Spud had taken a spark-striker from the gnarly man he had plundered.

The sparks betrayed their hiding place. But as men started toward them others nearer the airship sent up a howl of panic.

The lantern Soup threw had blown its reservoir. A merry fire was popping and crackling as it crawled toward the gas bladders. Would-be airship pirates fled. Some of the bolder tried to keep the burning oil contained. Those stalking toward Soup and Spud turned back.

Soup sent the second lantern arcing into the crowd. Meantime, Spud set a safer fire which sent up billows of dark smoke. "This is what I had in mind," he said. "Not attempted suicide."

"Yeah? Let's get out of here. We don't want to get rounded up with that lot. Too much explaining, I figure."

Avoiding capture, though, proved easier said than done. First, several very angry, determined, and per-severant gnarly men got onto their trail. Then soldiers popped up everywhere, sooner than expected.

The guilty officers, nervously alert, had heard the first uproar. They had decided to cover up. Three hundred soldiers were in the yards with orders to take no prisoners.

Unlike the pirates, Soup and Spud did not try to escape, only to evade. They lay low during the worst howl and clang. When it waned and the troops were feeling smug, they spied around and found a noncom known to themselves and Rider.

"Baracas," Soup called. "Over here." He stepped from the shadows skirting a mooring mast, into light where he could be recognized. Spud followed.

"You guys? What're you doing here?"

"Foiling an airship theft."

The soldier frowned. "That what was going on?"

"We rushed in on the courier from the Twelfth's camp on the Saverne side…" Soup shut up. Spud had gouged him.

The soldier, baffled, shrugged and said, "Stay close to me or you might get gutted with the rest. We'll let the tribunes sort you out later."

"That was the idea," Soup admitted.

The troops had the fires out. They were collecting bodies. Not a few wore imperial uniforms. The gnarly men and easterners were fierce when cornered. Soup counted a score of the squat men and nearly as many orientals. Spud observed, "This ought to break Shai Khe's back. He'll have to do his own dirty work now."

"How many got away?" Soup asked Baracas.

"None. That we know of."

Soup chuckled. "That'll get Shai Khe's goat. Can you imagine what he could have done with that airship? And his powers? He could have held the City hostage."

"Who the hell is this Shy Key?" Baracas asked.

"A villain with enough wealth to make your officers blind while forty men steal an imperial warship."

Baracas took them to the leading centurion of his maniple, who immediately kicked the question of their presence up to the tribune level.

They found officers gathered, discussing the excitement in secretive voices, when Baracas brought them to headquarters, near the yard gates. A sour-faced subaltern demanded, "What do you want, Baracas?"

"Sir, these men were mixing it up with the foreigners trying to steal the *Grand Phantom,* and I thought…"

"They were in there? What're they doing here? You had orders…"

"They're Rider's men, sir. They were trying to stop that gang."

A half dozen heads jerked around. Faces went pale. Someone muttered, "If the Protector is mixed up in this…"

A tribune moved closer. He snapped, "You! Baracas, is it? Why haven't you executed your orders?"

"Sir, they're Rider's…"

"Is Rider your superior officer? Kill them."

Soup grinned. "Now we know who'll be first to hang."

And Spud, "You do it, Baracas, and I'll bet you your pension you don't make it to sundown yourself."

Baracas grabbed him by the shoulder and shook him. He whispered, "Shut up! You want to get out of this alive?" The soldier was no fool. He had seen the lay of things.

Unfortunately, the tribune had, too. He drew a dagger. "Take them!"

Soup told Spud, "Brother, in this thing there's no end to the heads that need busted." He snatched up a camp stool.

Spud produced a knife taken from a fallen easterner. The officers closed in carefully. Those who knew the reputations of Rider and his men hung back, knowing a lot of people were going to get hurt.

Suddenly, darkness descended.

XXI

Rider stepped over the fallen tribune, knelt beside Spud, held an open phial beside his nose. He told Su-Cha, "Get the rest of these men tied."

Spud revived swearing and swinging. Rider plucked his fist out of the air. "Easy, Omar."

"Rider! How'd *you* get here?"

"Might ask you the same thing," Su-Cha chirruped. "You're supposed to be buried under a ruin on the Hurm Islands."

Soup reiterated Spud's behavior and question.

Su-Cha said, "We were thinking about rescuing you in a couple days. All that brainwork wasted."

"How come you're here, Rider?" Spud asked.

"We were tracking a creature that killed the chief of the King's Shadows. The trail passed near the military yards. We saw smoke. We arrived in time to see you being brought in here. Once the situation became clear, I used a knockout spell. Hurry, Su-Cha."

"We know why Shai Khe was in the area, now. And by now he must suspect his plan has gone sour. Let's find him before he gets away again. Omar. This soldier, Baracas. Do you trust him to keep this lot under arrest?"

"He knows what would happen to him if he didn't."

"Put him in charge, then. We have to go."

Minutes later they departed the military yards. Baracas came behind, leading the prisoners. All had been stripped of togas and badges of rank. They seemed a well-kempt chain of convicts. Baracas headed for the Citadel.

Rider headed toward the waterfront, along the yard fence.

"Look there," Soup said. "One of our eastern friends got away."

A man had dropped over the fence. He spotted them hastening toward him. His eyes got big. He whirled and ran.

Soup whooped and charged after him. Rider followed in a deceptive lope that ate ground fast. Over his shoulder, he told Su-Cha, "Get upstairs and follow him."

The imp stopped laboring to keep up. Soon he was a bird circling high above.

Rider snagged Soup's shoulder. "Let him lose us now."

Puffing, Soup glowered. "I'm not finished with those guys."

"He won't lead us while he can see us. If he loses us he'll run to his master."

And so it proved. Touching Rider through the web, Su-Cha reported their quarry moving more cautiously, watching his backtrail, yet now traveling with obvious purpose. Rider said, "Keep a sharp watch. Shai Khe will have sentries out."

That, too, proved true. But Rider's crowd kept them from reporting. They left a half dozen snoring thugs behind.

"This is the place," Rider said, staring at the blank face of a brick warehouse. Su-Cha circled above. "This time let's not let him get away." He dipped into his pockets, passed out what appeared to be green hens' eggs. He assigned posts around the warehouse. "Don't challenge him," he said. "If he comes your way, throw that, yell, and get under cover."

"What are they?" Spud asked.

Rider might not have heard. "Move out. I'll keep track through the web. I'm going inside on the count of a hundred."

The door through which the would-be airship pirate had fled stood ajar. Rider gave it a minute examination. It was as safe as it seemed. He slipped inside.

The warehouse was dark and seemed empty. The scurry of mice sent hollow clackings tumbling into the distance and back. Shai Khe was fond of dark places.

He slipped a green egg into each hand and advanced slowly. His eyes adjusted. Enough exterior light leaked in to permit navigation.

He heard a voice raised somewhere below, then the sounds of men moving hurriedly.

The fugitive had reported. His master was about to make his exit.

Rider ran, hunting a descending stairway.

He was too eager. He failed to notice a black silk trip line at ankle level. His toe hooked it.

He pitched forward, twisting. He hurled the egg in his right hand so he would not crush it when he broke his fall. He managed that in adequate silence, but the breaking egg sounded like a bottle smashing against pavement.

The sound was heard. Orders barked in an eastern tongue. Feet hammered on the steps. Rider ghosted into the concealment of a pillar. Three men pitched out of a shadow he had not recognized as a doorway. He flung his second egg.

It broke against a man's chest. The man flopped down immediately. The man behind him took three steps before collapsing. The third, to one side, halted in consternation. Rider leapt, felled him with one powerful punch.

Through the shadowed door and downstairs he loped—directly into a pair of guards with drawn blades.

He could not stop. It was too late. He flung himself through the air. His shout froze them for a second. A boot connected with a chin. A fist hammered the crown of a skull. Rider hit the floor and rolled, looking for more resistance.

A vast cellar surrounded him, dank and rank. There wasn't a soul to be seen.

A faint noise caught his ear. He hurried forward to a narrow canal leading into one wall of the basement. Shai Khe was escaping through the sewers!

The sound came again. It was the creak of an oar in an oarlock.

Rider extended himself through the web. The sewers were not well known to him. He traced them in his proximity. They formed a maze. He tried pinpointing Shai Khe, had no luck. The easterner used some clever sorcery to blind the web to his presence.

Had Rider had the proper tools he could have raised a spirit to set tracking Shai Khe, but he did not have the tools. The easterner had evaded him again.

Or had he? There was the thing Rider had been tracking when the uproar at the yards diverted him. Did Shai Khe's invisibility extend to it? It must be with its master.

He reached out, tugged at the web, took it in mental fingers, wove a net that would capture the whereabouts of the killing creature. And there it was! Moving away slowly, underground...

Rider raced upstairs, through the warehouse, into the bright street, touching his men as he went. They gathered quickly. "Shai Khe escaped into the sewers, but I'm tracking him through the web. Follow me."

His lope was deceptive. Soon even Chaz was puffing and straining.

Rider slowed till everyone caught up. He beckoned Su-Cha down. The imp perched on a balcony railing. Rider said, "Shai Khe is almost directly beneath us here. There is an outflow into the Bridge a few hundred yards away. There's nowhere else he can go."

"We going to jump him?" Chaz puffed.

"Yes. And don't hesitate an instant. He'll be ready. Don't take any needless risks, either." He loped off again. People paused to admire his swift, easy grace. He reached the outflow well before he expected Shai Khe.

The others joined him.

The outflow debouched between wharves. Small grain ships were tied up alongside each. Rider subjected them to a swift visual examination, saw nothing suspicious. He sent Soup and Spud aboard the nearest vessel on the right side, left Preacher and Chaz above the outflow, took Greystone aboard the vessel to the left. The masters of both ships protested.

A boat shot from the sewer mouth.

Eggs hailed against it. Rider hurled a grapnel appropriated aboard his ship. In a moment he was hauling the boat in. The sea breeze began to disperse the green mist hiding it.

"Where the hell is he?" Chaz shouted.

Shai Khe was not aboard.

The boat contained only an unconscious, shaggy, monkey-like thing slightly smaller than Su-Cha.

"Somewhere enjoying his joke at our expense," Rider said. He did not hide his disappointment.

XXII

Chaz tossed the shaggy assassin down onto the worktable in the laboratory. "What is it?" he asked Caracené.

She chewed her lip for a moment. "A khando. Their forebears were human. They lived in a city in the jungle in the east. One of their sorcerers overstepped himself a thousand years ago. A few generations later they had degenerated into near animals. They are just intelligent enough to be useful to Shai Khe."

"Well. A straight answer."

Rider completed a quick examination of the suite. The woman had done no damage. "You men get some rest. I'll look into the matter of Polybos House."

"What about our friends in the closet?" Preacher asked.

"Feed them. And the khando when it wakens. By

which time I suggest you have it caged."

Su-Cha snickered. He was studying the khando intently. Rider anticipated some devilment.

"I wonder if it could lead us to Shai Khe if we turned it loose," Chaz said.

"It might. And he'll be looking for that." Rider finished replenishing his pockets with oddities. "I'll be back soon. Try to restrain your propensities for finding trouble." He went to the door.

Behind him, Chaz growled, "Don't even think about it, runt. You shift into one of those, I'll break two necks just to make sure I get the right one."

"Always bullying. Do they send barbarians to school for that? One of these days... wham!"

The others began bickering about who had to feed the prisoners.

Rider smiled. They were handling the troublesome situation well.

King Belledon grumbled, "You took your good sweet time getting here."

"I had a chance to capture Shai Khe. It didn't work out, though. He had one more bolt hole than I could plug. You heard what happened in the yards?"

"Yes. I've been in a state of siege here. The Shadows have done everything but try to break in."

"Did Polybos House have anything to say?"

"Nothing. Neither accusations nor offers of pardon reach him. The more time passes, the more he seems in dread, though."

"His master does not have an easy way with followers who get themselves captured. Let me have a look at him."

House was isolated in a sitting room that could be entered by but one door. One of Belledon's nephews guarded that. The King carried the only key.

Rider did not recognize the bony human caricature called Polybos House. But House recognized him, and retreated in terror. Rider observed, "You judge all humanity by yourself." He settled into the room's one chair, stared at the prisoner. "Are you ready to talk?"

"*He* would kill me."

"Maybe. But won't he do that anyway? Isn't that what you expected from the beginning? And thought you could evade?"

House did not reply.

Rider was sure he had touched the truth, though. "Tell me about the Devil's Eyes."

House looked blank.

Rider said, "There is no way the King can overlook your treason. But you can get out of this with your skin if you help us take Shai Khe."

Still nothing.

"I don't understand this unreasoning fear of the man." He began tapping the fingernails of his right hand against the arm of his chair. When House still did not respond, he said, "I don't want to resort to a truth-drawing."

"There is no hope against *him*," House said. "He has half the world at his command. He has half of Shasesserre."

"He has very little of the City. I have taken it away. If he doesn't run soon..." Rider shifted subject. "Who were the most important men scheduled for assassination?"

Nothing.

There was a vaguely sagey, sweet smell in the air now. House began to look sleepy.

"General Partricus?" Rider asked. "His province is the east. I'd think Shai Khe would find him especially interesting. He returned to the City the other day. And he is a man beyond temptation or fear. If he hadn't those qualities he would not have received the eastern command."

Shasesserre, unlike some empires, was blessed with many devoted commanders.

House's eyes were almost shut. He nodded feebly. Then he started, glared at Rider suspiciously. Rider continued tapping his chair. House's eyes drifted shut.

Silent as death, Rider stalked closer. The sweet sage smell grew stronger. House began to snore.

Rider waited several minutes before breaking the seal on a small phial. He let House breathe the vapors that came forth. House wakened, but his eyes remained glazed.

Rider performed a series of small magicks. House became as stiff as a wooden statue.

Rider asked questions. House answered in a low, slow, flat voice, very literally. Rider had to phrase himself carefully to obtain answers filled with sense.

Even then he was not sure he had learned anything of value.

Polybos House had used the King's Shadows to advance Shai Khe's cause, but was not in the know in the easterner's organization. House mentioned names, but none were news to Rider. Every one had been in the book left by Vlazos. Those scheduled for assassination were no surprise either.

"The Devil's Eyes." Rider kept returning to that.

And getting nothing, no matter how he phrased his question.

Maybe there was no connection. Just random thoughts from the mind of a dying man.

Rider brought the King into the room. "I've gotten what little there is to be had. Keep him out of the way."

"You got nothing useful?"

"Very little. Shai Khe remains the key. I have to find him. Till I do we all have to stay alert. He'll keep trying."

XXIII

"So what do we do now?" Chaz asked. "He's outguessed us right down the line."

"He is here to eliminate men who threaten his imperialist dream. I've looked over the list of candidates for assassination. I want one of you to attach yourselves to each of the most likely. Excepting you, Su-Cha. I want you to shift again and fly around looking for places that might hide an airship."

"Come on!" Su-Cha protested. "You know how much energy shifting takes? You know how much a bird has to eat to keep going? My bones still ache from the last time. And I lost ten pounds. When you're my size you can't afford to lose ten pounds." He spun on Chaz, source of a volcanic, rumbling, mocking chuckle.

But it was Preacher who sank the spurs with a scriptural quotation about shirkers and malingerers.

"How does a guy get any respect around here?" Su-Cha demanded. "Without wearing a skirt? I'm the only one who's contributed anything in this business.

But do I get any appreciation? Oh, no! What I hear is a chorus of disdain from a bunch of losers."

Soup and Spud made violin noises. Squeaky violin noises. Only Greystone refrained from baiting the imp. Su-Cha glowered his way, expecting one of his rare but powerful jibes.

Chaz asked, "What're you going to do, Rider?"

"Barhop. And ask about the Devil's Eyes." He looked at the woman. "Do you have anything to report on the subject, Caracené?"

She shook her head.

Rider watched closely. He concluded that she knew nothing.

He did not understand women well. His life was too busy for them. But he knew the small twitches and evasions of eye that came with the slightest of lies, and believed women and men to be much alike in that respect.

He turned to his list of prospective murder victims. In a moment he began writing letters of introduction he hoped would place his followers near the men most at risk. He sent a man out as he completed each letter. The last gone, he began donning the disguise he would wear. Su-Cha watched. And ate.

The imp became bottomless when he did a lot of shifting, though in normal times he seldom ate at all. Su-Cha's metabolism was a mystery Rider could not penetrate. He suggested, "If you've learned the khando well enough, you might assume its shape. If the opportunity arises. After you have yanked the web to let me know where you are."

Su-Cha lifted a honey bun in salute. "My thoughts exactly."

Rider looked at the woman. "You're satisfied to be here?"

"I am safe here."

Rider betrayed no expression. But he wondered. "Su-Cha. Time. I'm ready, and I want to lock up behind me."

"Right. Any time." The imp grabbed two more buns. Once they had departed the room, he asked, "When are you going to rest, Rider?"

"I can't right now."

"A tired man makes mistakes."

"True. I haven't forgotten that."

"You think Shai Khe will run now? After the latest roundup?" The easterner's men from the warehouse had been collected by the City Guard.

"Not till he is under more pressure than we've managed so far. He should limit his ambitions, though."

"Later, then."

Rider watched Su-Cha rise and fly southward, toward the Golden Crescent. The warehouses were among the largest structures in Shasesserre. If Shai Khe were to hide an airship inside the City, he almost had to do so there.

Rider drifted into alleyways where he would have no trouble ambushing anyone following him. Setting several ambuscades yielded nothing. Finally, confident that he was not followed, he donned the rest of his disguise and returned to the streets as a Tiberian sailor. The hour was yet early for the taverns to bustle, but those that catered to sailors were busy enough. Rider faded in, looking as rough and fierce as the worst. A livid false scar, down his left cheek from temple to chin, leaving his left eye partially closed, lent him an especially piratic air.

A stranger in a sailors' bar dared not ask too many questions too directly. The distinction between merchant and smuggler was a matter of commercial or imperial viewpoint, and the crown was known for sending King's Shadows to look for customs evaders.

Rider, though, had a creditable story. He was hunting the man who had given him his scar, the man supposedly having struck him from ambush and left him for dead. He had come all the way from Tiberia seeking revenge. He had a perfect Tiberian accent, knew that land well having been there in service, and, as a Tiberian would on such a quest, he vacillated between frugality and offering drinks to anyone who might help him. The man he described to all listeners was Emerald.

Few Tiberians came as far east as Shasesserre. But other westerners sympathized with Rider's tale, and a few began accompanying him from one stew to another, seeking his mythical adversary.

He had been legitimized among the sailors.

In time he felt safe enough to insert questions about the Devil's Eyes.

Many a man had known Emerald, and none had become his friend. But no one recalled seeing him around lately.

The hunt widened as westerners with their own grievances began taking more active roles. Rider noted a growing uneasiness among eastern sailors, many of whom must have known who Emerald was and now feared being lumped together with him.

Rider suspected his imposture was getting out of hand.

It might have been the thirtieth tavern. He kept no count. But he was as alert as ever. He noted, amidst the rowdiness, one eastern face which remained quietly thoughtful. After a few minutes its owner began edging toward the door.

Before the man was halfway there Rider excused himself from his companions and headed for the rear of the tavern.

He ducked out the back and loped through the nearest breezeway to the street, arriving moments before the easterner marched past, oblivious to watching ayes.

Rider shed most of his disguise. He tore his sailor's clothing, making himself look less prosperous. He slipped a pebble into a shoe, donned a stoop, and set out after the easterner.

Rider's precautions were wasted. The sailor was not concerned about his backtrail. He merely meant to report news probably of minimal interest.

The trail, inevitably, led toward water. Toward the river again. It seemed Shai Khe had to have water at his back. As he hurried through the gathering shadows, Rider pondered the significance of that.

He reached through the web and touched his men. Without exception he found them bored. Then he reached for Su-Cha.

He found the imp perched among the gargoyles surrounding the statue of an old king atop a commemorative pillar facing the sea the king had conquered. Su-Cha had assumed the shape of a gargoyle. He was sleeping.

Rider nudged him.

The imp squawked and launched himself from

the pillar, to the astonishment of witnesses below. He filled the web with conflicting excuses for his having taken a nap.

Rider ignored them all. *Come help me follow a man,* he sent. Disguise or no, his continued presence behind the man he stalked meant ever-increasing risk of discovery, especially as the gathering night made it necessary to remain close.

Su-Cha arrived quickly. His night vision was superb. Rider drifted back.

The stalk led up the bank of the river, beyond the water gate and wall, and then past suburbs into marshes where country folk hunted waterfowl and gathered wild rice. The easterner seemed well acquainted with the path he followed through the boggy land.

Su-Cha dropped down to confer with Rider, who followed a safe quarter mile behind. "He's probably heading for an old hulk that's on the river's edge over yonder," the imp said. "The trail is hard to spot from up there. But I did notice two places where men like that Emerald are hanging around. Good ambush places."

Rider gave the imp two green eggs. "Drop these on them after the man goes past. Wait for me outside the hulk."

Su-Cha grunted and flapped away.

An hour later Rider met the imp a hundred yards from the hulk, which loomed like the corpse of a beached whale against the night. Su-Cha said, "I think we and our friend have had a long walk for nothing."

"How's that?"

"Right after I egged the first ambush I noticed a boat leaving the hulk. Headed downriver. I'm pretty sure Shai Khe was in it."

"Uhm." Rider stared at the hulk.

"Do we hit it anyway? Take it away, too?"

"Did those men seem suspicious before they fell asleep?" He had slipped past both sets of guards without bothering either.

"I don't think so."

"Then we'll leave things be. For now. Except to add a few flourishes." In his pockets Rider carried several stones, cousins to that through which he had tracked Soup and Spud. He showed them to Su-Cha, who grinned as much as he could with a beak. Then the imp began changing shape.

He became one of the huge semi-aquatic rodents that inhabited the marshes, a beast variously called a waterbear, a waterdog, or a waterrat. The creatures were known for their curiosity, stupidity, and a fearlessness based primarily on the fact that their flesh was so tough and ill-flavored even a crocodile avoided eating them. The men aboard the hulk would be accustomed to occasional inspections by itinerant waterbears.

Su-Cha filled his rat mouth with Rider's stones.

Ten minutes later the hulk reverberated to shouts of exasperation. Five minutes more and Su-Cha had returned, grinning. He changed again. "I marked most of them."

Rider sensed the stones through the web. "Their movements should tell us a lot. Let's get back to the City. Shai Khe will be up to some deviltry."

XXIV

Chaz had been told to guard Lord Priscus Procopio. Procopio was a retired general who had won distinction in the far east. He had won many new provinces, and the hearts of the people who dwelt in them. He had shown no mercy to the old cults and tyrants that had oppressed and tortured those lands.

Now Procopio was a leading royal adviser. And Rider assumed he was a man familiar with the threat posed by the sinister Shai Khe.

Indeed he was. "We crossed swords twice, out in Nuna," he told Chaz, as they looked out over Shasesserre from behind heavy glass. "He was old and cunning even then. Lucky for me he hadn't the reputation he's got now. The people out there exposed his plots both times. The second time I caught and executed his son. Or a man purported to be his son."

"Then you really believe he's trouble, eh?"

"Of course."

"'Bout time we ran into somebody who does." Chaz knew Soup and Preacher had been refused access to the men they were supposed to guard, and that the others had gotten only slightly more cooperation from their charges.

"I'll believe anything I hear about Shai Khe. The man is a devil. I've seen the wretches who have escaped his rule. I've talked to them. And I know I'm near the top of his hate list, because of his son. Shasesserre itself must bear that hatred, so long as he lives. No, I don't doubt anything. And I'm terrified."

Chaz said, "You don't look it."

"You learn to tame fear, and mask it, when you're a proconsul trying to rule twenty millions and you're backed only by five thousand swords and a few airships. You learn to appear as indifferent as stone. If the dogs sense so much as an apprehension in you, you're lost."

Chaz scanned the lights of the great City. Even after years he was not comfortable here. "And is there a point to it? To the army being in Nuna, I mean. Is there a mutual benefit?"

Procopio's expression soured. "Until the magnates and tax farmers feel it's tamed enough to move in. Even then, I suppose. Our reign isn't nearly so fearful as that we displaced."

A foreigner himself, Chaz vacillated between viewpoints on the benefits of imperial rule. Some were obvious, like freedom from continual intertribal warfare. But they seemed balanced by losses less tangible.

"Ach!"

"What?" Procopio demanded.

"Someone in the street. Passed through the light coming from yonder window. He was only there for a second, but I'd bet it was Shai Khe. Moved that snaky way he has."

Procopio shuddered. "Think he'll use sorcery?"

"No. That would get Rider hot on his trail."

"It'll be something cunning and unexpected, then."

"Better be *very* sneaky. Or he's had it." The entire household was alert. Nevertheless, Chaz began another circuit of the darkened room, seeking weaknesses hitherto overlooked.

There were only two possible points of entry, other than a direct smash through the massive window.

A faint drone came from the mouth of the fireplace. It put Chaz in mind of a beehive wakening.

The big barbarian grinned. For this he was prepared.

On a table nearby were several earthenware jars in the amphora shape but only eight inches tall. Each was sealed with a thin layer of wax. From the wax protruded a wick. He lighted one of these from a small candle hitherto concealed within a cabinet. He placed the jar in the fireplace. He and Procopio both drew deep breaths and buried their faces in balls of moistened cotton.

The jar suddenly sent flames and gases roaring up the flue. The fire blasted thirty feet up from the chimney's head.

The flue filled with a brief flutter, then a rattle. Chaz lowered the candle, watched scores of giant bees rain down upon the hearthstone. Each was dead, wingless, roasted, poisoned.

Chaz grinned wickedly in the candlelight. He beckoned Procopio. "Come on."

The old soldier was spry enough to keep pace with Chaz's wild charge for the hatch that gave access to the roof. He snatched an old war axe off a wall along the way, a trophy from some campaign of his younger years.

The two erupted onto the roof in time to see a silhouette vanish over the edge. Another lay beside the chimney.

Fearless of the height, Procopio dashed to the edge. He hefted his axe and paused, as if timing… Down the weapon went, hurled. A yell attested to the accuracy of his throw.

Chaz knelt beside the form lying against the chimney. The man's face was gone. He must have been looking down the chimney when Chaz had sprung his surprise.

Beside him lay an ovoid box, which proved to house a paper nest.

"Nasty thing," Procopio said. "Saw them out east. Their sting can fell a mule. Worst part is, they can be trained. Never heard of using a whole nest before, though. Guess Shai Khe wanted to make sure."

Chaz straightened, stared down at the patch of light spilling from the window across the way. A tall, lean form glided into it. Its eyes glowed greenly. It bowed slightly, then moved away.

Hastily, Chaz dragged out a knife and hurled it. It rang upon stone. An almost mischievous chuckle floated upward. Chaz cursed. "Let's get after him."

The old soldier restrained him. "He would like nothing better. Stay. Savor the triumph we've achieved."

XXV

All through the night assassins moved. They were not many, but their ways were stealthy and cunning. Never were they so direct or crude as to employ frontal attack with steel.

They struck in six places in addition to making the attempt on Procopio. Rider guessed well enough to have sent men to four of the slated victims. Not one man died who had the wit to accept protection from one of Rider's men. Both men who refused it perished.

Rider himself reached the City too late to participate in anything but the mourning.

"Four men dead." For the first time since the affair began his anger threatened to betray him. He had driven himself to the limit of his astonishing physical resources. "One more imposition, Su-Cha. One more change. Patrol above the river. High up. See if Shai Khe's boat returns to that hulk."

Weariness and reaction to the murders had sapped the imp's spirit. He voiced none of his customary complaints. He simply nodded.

Rider said, "I'll be waiting at the airship yards."

Su-Cha went up into the night. Rider gathered his men and led them to the yards, where they boarded his favorite fast airship. They all collapsed into exhausted sleep.

Su-Cha arrived as Rider wakened, alerted by the imp's tug on the web. "He's there," Su-Cha gasped, and collapsed.

Rider wakened his men. They gaped at the imp, for this was the first time they had seen him sleep.

"Take your stations," Rider said. He alerted the airship's motive demon. Then he described what he and Su-Cha had discovered while the others were, for the most part, trying to save the lives of men who refused to believe themselves endangered.

"We could be seen lifting off," Greystone cautioned.

"I intend operating on the assumption that we will be," Rider replied. "But we'll feint to the east, up the Bridge. In any event, the ship can outrun any messenger."

The airship came out of the east, with the rising sun. It hurtled over the marshes so low the belly of the gondola whispered to the touch of tall reeds. Below, waterbears squeaked in sudden fright. Yawning marsh crocodiles bellowed in amazement and slithered into the safety of their deep pools.

Startled Emerald-like sentries gawked, then shouted warnings that were far too late.

The hulk loomed ahead. Rider lifted the airship a dozen feet and slowed it. His men sent canisters tumbling down...

A noxious violet miasma enveloped the decaying ship.

Su-Cha, who had wakened only moments before, put into words what only Rider had noticed. "The boat. It's gone."

Sullen grumbles greeted the news.

Rider backed and lowered the airship, dropped Chaz and Preacher. The purple fog had dissipated already.

The two were back in minutes. "Nobody there," Chaz reported as he clambered aboard.

Rider nodded as he began making altitude, looking for a boat. The stones Su-Cha had planted were still alive. And still aboard the hulk. Shai Khe had detected their emanations and had known his hideout stood betrayed.

No suspicious boat plied the river. Shai Khe could not have gone far, for he hadn't had time. Rider doubted he could have reached the hulk long before the airship's arrival.

The eastern sorcerer had a sixth sense for peril, that was certain. He hadn't bothered wasting time setting booby traps. He had gotten while a chance to get remained.

"Back to square one again," Greystone said.

"Hardly," Preacher countered. "Hardly at all." He handed Rider a sheet of paper.

Rider moved nearer a window and stared at the sheet a long time. Finally, he handed it to Greystone.

The scholar grunted. "Il Diavolo. From the nether shore."

Chaz looked over Greystone's shoulder. "Looks like Shroud's Head to me. Pretty good drawing, for charcoal."

"It is Shroud's Head. But when King Shroud had it sculpted, the slaves who did the work called it Il Diavolo. The Devil. The island sea peoples, they gave Shroud that name after he beat them off Klotus, then made them commemorate the defeat by carving the cliff into a face that would watch them forever."

Chaz said, "That means that fishing boat was going somewhere after all."

Rider nodded. "That's possible."

Shroud's Head had been carved from a two-hundred-foot-high promontory just miles down the Bridge from where Rider had had the guardship intercept the boat that had carried away Soup and Spud.

"The Devil's Eyes," Spud mused. "One of them is a cave, isn't it?"

Rider nodded. "Big enough to conceal a small airship."

"What're we waiting for?" Chaz demanded. "Let's go get them."

"Haste is not indicated," Greystone scolded.

"He's right," Rider said. "A clue like this is almost too sweet a find. For the moment we'd better assume it was left deliberately. Instead of rushing into a trap, let's see if we can't entangle Shai Khe in his own snare. In any event, we can close that door when we want. For now we'll concentrate on thwarting his assassins."

Rider started the airship down river in a not very hopeful search, leaving the hulk burning behind. After a few minutes, he said, "We've won one victory, of sorts. We've forced him to abandon his designs on the City. To lower himself to the spiteful murder of fancied enemies."

"Kind of understating there," Greystone observed.

"Possibly. Our job now is to take away his killing game. To compel him to come at us head to head."

"Wonderful," Chaz said. "That's what I've been waiting for all my life. A chance to go one on one with a guy so bad he scares himself when he walks past a mirror."

"We can handle him," Rider promised. "And while he's preoccupied with us he won't have time for anybody else."

Chaz grumbled a lot.

As Rider expected, they found no sign of Shai Khe's boat.

XXVI

Between them, Rider and his men had hundreds of friends and acquaintances in all walks of life and at every stratum of society. Most notably at the lowest stratum, where the dark deeds and secret things are known, and the wicked deeds are done. Rider had the word go out at all levels, with a promise of a substantial reward where that might count: the Protector's son wanted information about certain easterners who might have been involved in his father's murder.

The Protector's death was a secret no more. And much of the City was aware that strange doings were afoot. The news of the murder had come out slowly, to a populace already certain something bad had occurred. There was tension and apprehension, but no panic.

Most people believed Rider could assume the Protector's mantle. He was Jehrke's son and Jehrke had trained his boy to step into his shoes. This crisis would test the temper of the sword that Jehrke had forged.

Chaz thought the whole business had turned hilarious. "Those guys are the ones on the spot now," he crowed. "They stick their heads out anywhere and they're had."

Rider watched the woman Caracené hover around the barbarian. "I'm uncomfortable being dependent on the help of others. We have to remain self-sufficient. There will be many times, in years to come, when we will have no other resources."

Greystone countered, "Your father himself said to use the tools at hand. In this case I think the threat justifies an appeal to the people."

The others were a bit puzzled. They were not used to seeing Rider doubt himself.

Rider said, "I expect Shai Khe to make a gesture before long. A show of force, if you will, to demonstrate that he can move at will even in reduced circumstances. Chaz, you'd better go back to General Procopio." He also assigned men to Soup, Spud, and Su-Cha.

"What about me and Greystone?" Preacher complained. "Are you cutting us out?"

"You hold the fort. Keep track of whatever reports come in. If anything comes in that looks especially good, investigate if you like. Don't start anything with Shai Khe. Just keep an eye on him."

Looking at Caracené with an odd glint in his eye, Chaz smacked a fist into a palm and said, "I'd like to lay something more than an eye on that wheezer."

"Where are you going to be?" Su-Cha asked. Already Rider was adopting one of his many disguises.

As he often did when he did not wish to answer a direct question, Rider developed a sudden deafness.

Those who were to go out on guard duty began collecting items they might need. No one pressed Rider when he did not want to talk.

They watched in awe as he prepared himself. It was amazing just how much he could secrete about his person.

XXVII

Rider and the others had not been gone twenty minutes when there was a pounding at the door. Trusting no one, Preacher concealed himself within the device of mirrors and covered Greystone.

Greystone looked through the periscope peephole. "It's an officer of the King's bodyguard." He unlocked the door "What can I do for you?"

The officer looked embarrassed. "The King insists you guys should take charge of the prisoner Polybos House. His Majesty isn't up to all the fuss and bother."

Greystone scowled. There were moments when he was not too fond of his sovereign. "I guess we can throw him in with the others. Which reminds me. They're overdue to be fed."

Preacher groaned from concealment. It was his turn to make the meal.

The officer said, "The sergeant of the guard said to tell you he's got a bunch of reports for you guys down in his office. Everyone in town wants a piece of that reward. They're lined up at the gate."

"I'll go down while you're getting House."

Greystone was astonished. Four harried scribes were taking statements as fast as they could write. They had completed a stack of reports nearly a foot high. "We didn't expect this," he told the sergeant of the guard.

"It's just getting started. Take a look outside."

Greystone looked. There must have been two hundred people waiting. Quite a few wore shantor's robes.

That made sense. Both Jehrke and Rider had done their best to help victims of the weeping sickness.

"I'll come back down as soon as we've digested these," Greystone promised, scooping up the stack already prepared.

"Anything strange happened around here lately?" Chaz asked as he joined General Procopio. The general was in his study again. Chaz noted that several meticulously mounted giant bees had been added to the old soldier's collection of memorabilia.

"Been as quiet as a mouse's fiftieth birthday party." Procopio moved to the window.

"Mice don't live..." Chaz reddened.

"Unless you count the shantors." Procopio pointed.

Chaz watched as two victims of the weeping sickness moved slowly past the house.

Procopio observed, "They usually don't beg this neighborhood."

Chaz grunted. "Bet they usually ring their warning bells, too."

"And they don't keep shuffling around the same block."

"Maybe we should go down and give them some alms."

Procopio put on a big grin. There was a lot of adventure left in that old soldier. "Maybe."

The shantors Spud encountered *were* ringing their bells. They seemed old and advanced in their disease. They moved at a snail's pace, leaning upon their staffs heavily. "Alms?" one croaked hopefully as Spud came up.

Spud reached into a pocket.

And the instant his hand was engaged the shantor on his right swung his staff.

Spud managed to evade that blow but not the one coming in from his left. That fake shantor tapped him over the ear. He sagged into the grasp of his attackers.

Bystanders gawked. Then they began shouting. Someone had recognized Spud and reasoned that these fake shantors must belong to the gang Rider was hunting.

But there were few bystanders, and none of them armed well enough to overcome two villains skilled with staffs. The shantors dragged Spud away.

The two who tried to take Soup were less fortunate. Bystanders overcame them. In moments they were trussed up and on their way to cells in the Citadel. Soup was on his way, too. He whistled. But now he was more alert.

The shantors outside the Citadel gate were not ringing their bells. They had been, but with so much enthusiasm that the sergeant of the guard had ordered them to stop.

They were very nervous. Their master had ordered out every man he had left on what seemed to be a desperate last gamble. One man, more bold than the others, dared say, "This is a pretty savvy plan. We go charging into the Citadel so we don't inconvenience anybody by making them drag us here from halfway across town."

"Shut up and listen for the signal."

The sergeant of the guard was never sure if the shrill whistle came from behind him or from outside. He would never forget exactly what happened next, though.

A mob of shantors poured through the gate, clubbing guards, would-be reward collectors, and scribes. He managed to cut one attacker with his shortsword, then his lights went out.

The gang split into two parties. One went upstairs. The other went down, toward cells where many of their associates were confined. As fate would have it, the latter group took a wrong turn, became lost for five minutes, and when they found their way again also found that they had used up too much time. Soldiers and jailors fell upon them while they were opening the cells.

What followed was a merry roughhouse.

The invaders did not get the best of it.

"It's that captain and House and a couple of soldiers," Greystone said from the peephole. He opened the door.

The soldiers started House through…

A wave of shantors hit them from behind.

Greystone, House, the captain, and the soldiers went down under the tide.

Preacher shot one man and brained another with his crossbow before the rush made a shambles of his hiding place. Then he was trying to defend himself against clubs with bare hands. He got in a few good licks before he fell.

He lay there in semi-consciousness while the raiders located Caracené, the prisoners, and the hairy man-ape. Going into and returning from the suite the raiders gave Jehrke a superstitiously wide berth. They kept yelling at one another to hurry.

Hands grabbed Preacher up. He saw Greystone lifted, and Caracené…

After that there was a lot of confusion. A lot of fighting, in which a lot of Citadel folk seemed to be helping the raiders and getting killed for their trouble.

Then one of the men carrying Preacher got bashed in the face with a pike butt. His partner dropped Preacher and ran for it.

Preacher's world went watery for a while.

A vigorous shaking wakened Preacher. He swore, then admonished himself with a scriptural quotation. He opened his eyes.

It took him a moment to recognize the man shaking him. The fellow had blood in his hair and all over his face. It was the captain who had tried to deliver Polybos House. The captain asked, "Are you all right?"

"I'll probably live. Worse luck. Did we get them all?"

"Maybe a dozen got away." The captain looked around. "Really brought all the rats out of the walls this time. Your eastern friend played every counter he had. And used most of them up."

"That seemed an awful lot of trouble just to rescue Polybos House."

The captain laughed a hard laugh. "Rescue him? He's the first one they killed."

"Then what?…"

"The woman. That ape thing. You and your sidekick. But I think mainly the woman."

Preacher tried to get up. The pounding in his head forced him back down. "Greystone?"

"Took him with them."

The first reports began to filter in soon afterward. No one was stopping the raiders—they were moving faster than the news—but their every step was noted. Their path—of course—led directly to the river.

XXVIII

Rider noticed the men tailing him immediately. There were three of them and they were fairly good, but he spotted them all the same. He shook them by a method that was almost cruel.

He began running, confident none of his pursuers could stay with him all the way to his destination.

The toughest kept up for five miles.

Rider ran five more miles, at a slower pace. By then he was well into the farm country west of Shasesserre. He ducked into a woodlot and adjusted his disguise slightly. When he reappeared upon the road he looked to be just another farm laborer trudging along with hands thrust into pockets.

His trudge was deceptive. It ate ground quickly. And when he was sure no one was watching he ran.

It was the hard way to make this journey. The slow way. But Shai Khe's spies and eyes would not be watching for a man afoot. An airship or a dromon, yes. Perhaps chariots, coaches, or horsemen. But not a lone, stooped, tired farm hand.

At dusk he came to the ridge that formed the spine of Shroud's Head. He was more than forty miles from the Citadel. That much walking tired even him. He located a sheltered place and fell asleep immediately.

He wakened six hours later, in the ebb hour of the night, exactly as planned. He listened to cricket sounds. Nothing else was moving, a fact he confirmed by cautious extension of his wizard's senses.

Confident that he was alone and unwatched, he began working his way up and out the ridge. He avoided trails and easy traveling. In the dark even the most skilled of men could overlook some warning device.

He reached the crown of Shroud's Head without incident or discovery. Once there he settled himself and set his wizard's senses roaming in earnest.

There were guards, yes. And warning devices. And an incredibly complex net of spells meant both as alarm and trap... And something more. Something dark, the nature of which he could not immediately discern.

There were only two men, though. One was asleep and the other was nodding. There should have been more. Unless Shai Khe had grown so short of manpower he had stripped his airship of its crew.

That must be it. Rider could detect no other human beings anywhere within reach of his talent.

That other thing, though... He had begun to sense its outlines, its black formless form. And he had begun to suspect what it might be. And if it was, he had learned much about the horror that slithered within a man named Shai Khe.

If that thing were loosed, no single sorcerer, not even a Jehrke or a Shai Khe, would be able to bind it again. An army would be needed, and many of them would die in the struggle. Horribly. But for now it was confined and constrained and could, with relative ease, be returned to that foul place whence it had been summoned.

If Rider could untangle the net of spells shielding both airship and devil.

Now he knew why Kralj Odehnal had said "Devil's Eyes" instead of "Devil's Eye." The deep cave and hidden airship were only half the story. There was, perhaps, the approximation of a pun in confining the devil in the other, shallower eye.

Rider examined the nest of spells. His regard for Shai Khe, as a sorcerer, rose. It would be a long, arduous, interesting, dangerous job, penetrating that without leaving tracks. He settled in to do it.

He was through. He was safely inside unseen. He had done what he had come to do and had seen what he had come to see. And now he was trapped.

Just as he was about to leave, Shai Khe's airship crew returned, having come down the Bridge of the World by boat. And with them they had brought Caracené, Soup, and Greystone. How had they gotten to Greystone and the girl?

For the moment all three were safe enough. The airshipmen had orders to install them in the airship and keep them confined. Nothing more.

Rider wished he could get back to the City and learn what had happened. The airshipmen knew nothing. But he could not depart without being seen, or, at least, without leaving traces that would be instantly apparent to Shai Khe's eye.

He slipped into a shadowed cleft and rested, and waited for a chance to make a properly discreet departure.

XXIX

"The boat just vanished?" Chaz demanded, keeping one eye on General Procopio, who had his nose into everything in the laboratory. The general was as excited as a kid. Retirement had been a bore for him. "Right in the middle of the river?"

Preacher nodded. He was tired of repeating the story.

"Then he used sorcery. Meaning he was willing to disturb the web and attract attention."

"Like maybe he hadn't been noticed so far?" Su-Cha sneered. "The boat only had to disappear for a couple minutes. Just long enough to get to shore and let those guys do a fade."

Chaz paced. He was concerned about Caracené, though torture would not have gotten him to admit that. He stared at the darkness beyond the laboratory window. The gruesome memorial that had been Jehrke Victorious watched over his shoulder. "Where is the boss?"

"Gone. Without saying where he was going. The way he does."

Chaz stared at the vermilion characters in the window glass. They had, according to Preacher, simply appeared while his back was turned.

Ride-Master Jehrke: You no longer possess the pearl so precious to me. I now possess two gems priceless to you.

"What do we do now?" Chaz asked.

"We wait," Preacher said.

General Procopio was stirring through wreckage left from the recent raid. "What is *this* thing?" He indicated something that looked like a mummified gorilla head. "Ugly character."

"No telling," Chaz replied. "Jehrke had at least one of everything weird there ever was around here."

Su-Cha scooted past the barbarian. "Don't touch that!" he squeaked.

Procopio jerked away. Startled, Chaz asked, "What's the matter, little buddy?"

"That's nothing Rider or Jehrke ever had. That's a Koh-Rehn. We've been double-shuffled. Those clowns that broke in here left it for us. A little gift. A little nightmare come midnight, while you're all tucked safely into your beds, you think." He squatted beside the ugly head, studying it.

"Relative of yours?" Procopio asked, catching on more quickly than the others.

"In a manner of speaking." After a thoughtful moment, Su-Cha said, "Dirty tricks, eh, Shai Khe?" And after another moment, "We can play that game, too. Listen up, you guys. I've got an idea."

Midnight. A blinding flash lighted the window of Jehrke's laboratory. Tough though the glass there was, it disintegrated, showering the Rock with fragments. Roars and screams ripped out into the night. A man who might have been Ride-Master Jehrke could, for a moment, be seen battling a huge shadow. Then the screaming stopped.

One minute. Two minutes. Three. Two battered men fled the Citadel gate, a semi-conscious woman dragging between them. As they neared the edge of the plaza, the shorter man stumbled. He let go the woman to break his fall. The shawl wrapping the woman's hair and concealing her features fell away.

"Damnit!" Chaz exploded, but softly. "Watch yourself. They find out we've still got her, we lose our chance to pull this out without Rider." He re-wrapped the woman while Preacher muttered weary apologies.

They resumed hurrying through the night, following a circuitous path that in time led them to a new hideout at General Procopio's City house. The general had insisted. He wanted to be in the middle of things, and the Protector himself had proofed the house against sorcerous espionage. He said. Where better to stake out the goat and wait for the lion? he asked.

There were fragile indications to convince Chaz that they were being followed. He allowed himself one merry grin.

Good times and bad, chaos or disorder, there were comings and goings at the Citadel gate. Day, night, the hour made no matter.

A curtained coach departed twenty minutes after Chaz and Preacher and their charge. Within were Spud, Procopio, and a stack of reports from the sergeant of the guard, who had not permitted a little thing like a raid to cancel his report-taking.

The coach hurried through the night, straight to Procopio's back gate, and so arrived there long before the others did afoot. They were in the darkened study, watching, to confirm the presence or absence of trackers when Chaz and Preacher arrived.

Those two burst in with their burden. "Well?" Chaz boomed as Su-Cha surrendered the Caracené shape and collapsed with a feeble plea for food.

"Two of the bloody beggars," Procopio replied. "One ran away to tell tales. One stayed."

"We ought to sneak out the back way and follow him home to Daddy," Chaz growled.

Spud, trying to spoon-feed Su-Cha in the dark, said, "We already know where to find Daddy."

"What? How?"

"All those reports the sergeant gave me? While you guys were loafing I was reading. There's wheat in amongst all that chaff, and it adds up to another waterfront warehouse. While we were killing time giving you guys a head start, the general called in some favors. As soon as Shai Khe's gang heads out, wherever, they'll hit the place and get Soup, Greystone, the girl, and whoever is guarding them. Then they'll lay for Shai Khe in case he gets lucky or gets away out here."

Chaz grunted. It was an eloquent grunt, replete with sarcasm and cynicism. "And it all depends on Rider being somewhere handy, looping snares and nets into the web for when Shai Khe cuts loose, eh? Ingenious."

Preacher quoted something scriptural; predictably cryptic and confused; fierce, fiery, and deifically vengeful. He added, "It's falling together. We have that rat in the middle, between two terriers, and we'll choke him on his own arrogant overconfidence."

Perhaps the word *choke* occurred to him because of the strangling noises issuing from Su-Cha because Spud kept jabbing too-rapid spoonfuls of food into the imp's mouth. Su-Cha finally got his message through. He was recovering. He was ready for the next stage.

They began their wait for the mad enemy.

XXX

When the alarms went off there was a tinge of grey in the night beyond the nose of the pirate airship. Men bolted to their weapons. There was panic in the air. The airshipmen's morale was low.

It was not about to improve.

A man appeared outside, hands raised, yelling at them to restrain themselves, that he was on their side, that he had a message, that they were to let him come inside.

They let him in. Not because he insisted but because some of the crew recognized him. Immediately he began chattering in a clicky tongue Rider recognized but could not follow. His message was received with groans and outrage.

A sleepy crewman leaned out of the airship gondola and demanded, in a language Rider could follow, "What's all the racket?"

One of the others replied, "The Celestial Lord wishes us to put our guests back on the boat and take them back to the City. Right now."

Puzzled, Rider watched preparations being made. When the airshipmen brought their "guests" forth he began to get a glimmer. Whatever had happened in the City, some of his associates had survived to counterattack. Through guile.

Caracené had arrived under loose, indulgent restraint, like a wayward child being shepherded home.

She was departing in bonds, hung about with every piece of silver the airshipmen could muster. She went silently, aware that protest was useless and time the sole cure for this indignity.

Rider permitted himself a rare grin. Somehow, Su-Cha had convinced Shai Khe that Caracené might in fact be a certain nimble-witted, shape-shifting imp.

The airshipmen hustled their prisoners out of the cave. Before they disappeared, Rider was at work preparing his own unnoticed departure.

A spell of minor scale—the one he had employed to escape the Treasury vaults—blinded the stay-behinds to his presence. He then turned to Shai Khe's network of protective and detective spells. He saw instantly that slipping through would be easy. All the hectic in and out of airshipmen, prisoners, and messenger had left the magical artifact in a state of vibrant dissonance. It was a moment's work to confuse his own passage with that of those ahead of him.

A narrow, steep pathway descended the face of Shroud's Head. From a ship on the Bridge it looked like the thin scar that appeared on the faces of all the old king's statues and busts.

Rider reached the head of the path only minutes behind the others. They were just two hundred yards ahead. But he was stumped.

The pathway slanted down to a wooden jetty that would be invisible from the shipping lanes. Tied up to it was a small smuggler's ship with mast unstepped. From the Bridge it might look like a rock.

Rider's immediate concern was the fact that the pathway appeared to be the only way to reach the ship. Or was it?

He set his mystic senses roaming.

There were handholds enough for a descent, but that way would be slow. And, shadow spell or no, he would be seen if exposed to enemy eyes that long. However...

The alternative appeared mad even for a man as remarkable as Rider. He cast his senses again. And hesitated not an instant.

He retreated into the cave as far as he dared, took several quick, deep breaths, sprinted forward—right out into the nothing of a two-hundred-thirty-foot drop to the waters of the Bridge.

Shadow flickered around him. His plunge went unremarked—till he hit water a dozen feet from the jetty.

The airshipmen halted and gabbled at one another about the tremendous splash. Several of the more daring hurried ahead.

Rider's collision with the face of the sea left him stunned for a few seconds. Then he realized he was going deeper than he wanted, dragged down by the mass of gewgaws he carried. He swam upward with powerful kicks and armstrokes, slanting so as to surface beneath the jetty. He rose, gulped air, clung to a float just long enough to dispose of such devices as would have been ruined by the water. Then he went under again, stroking under the smuggling craft.

The ship was long and narrow and had a very low freeboard. Rider grasped the gunwale amidships, levered himself aboard. The spell of shadows guarded him from the eyes of the forerunner airshipmen, who were approaching the foot of the path. He slipped into shadows beneath a raised foredeck. Before concealing himself within a pile of old tackle and sailcloth he flung a small spell across the deck and gunwale. The dampness there evaporated.

The three leading airshipmen clumped aboard the smuggler, grumbling. They had decided the splash had been caused by a rock falling off the face of Shroud's Head.

Within minutes the entire complement had boarded. The ship got under way.

XXXI

With Chaz and General Procopio more or less running the show, the welcome planned for Shai Khe was about as subtle and gentle as a sledge hammer.

Chaz was not a man to use a rapier where a battleaxe would do.

But it seemed the battleaxe would not get taken in hand.

It was not that long a wait before shadows began flitting about outside. There was even a moment when one of those solidified into the devil shape of Shai Khe, calmly assessing the house. But the easterner was not to be taken easily. Whether or not he believed Rider dead, he would not abandon caution. Nothing else happened.

When dawn came the watchers retreated. There was never any doubt of their nearby presence, though. Each few hours Su-Cha assumed Caracené's form and showed himself at a window, casting longing looks toward liberty.

"I wish he'd *do* something!" Chaz growled.

"He is," Preacher rejoined. "He's working on your

mind. In a little while he'll have you charging out where he can bang your head all day long."

Chaz scowled but refused the bait. "We're the guys laying in the weeds. What's he waiting for?"

"He smells a rat," the general said. "The man has a nose for danger. The gods alone know how many times he slipped my snares out east."

Su-Cha guessed, "He's waiting for the real Caracené, I'll bet. I'll bet he sent her out of the City, then had to have her brought back to make sure she isn't me."

"So we didn't accomplish anything."

"Sure we did. We bought time for Rider to finish whatever he's doing and get back into the lists here. While we've had Shai Khe tied down accomplishing nothing himself. We got rid of all but a handful of his thugs. If the general's pals have held up their end, we've grabbed off his hideout behind him. When he goes running back…"

"Yeah? You're forgetting something, runt. If he figures Rider is croaked, the only thing keeping him from popping the cork on Shasesserre is the chance we've still got the woman. Whatever she means to him."

"Yes," Preacher said, peeping out the corner of the window. "We've got some action coming."

They all crowded the window. Below, an oriental horseman galloped toward the house. A pair of City Guardsmen pursued him, bellowing. Their words could not be distinguished, but it seemed they wanted the oriental to desist from his reckless behavior.

All three passed without slowing.

A minute went by.

Men began to appear as if from nowhere. One was Shai Khe himself. They departed at a brisk pace.

"One watcher each, front and back, I would guess," Chaz said. "Get out there and do your stuff, little buddy."

Su-Cha grinned. "Ever notice how I get to be his buddy when he wants me to stick my neck out?" But already he was shifting form, as they had made it up ahead.

They had no trouble with Shai Khe's men, who had not foreseen danger in the guise of a cute little boy. Besides the immediate watchers, the easterner left two sentries along his backtrail. His path led straight to the warehouse Preacher had identified as Shai Khe's current headquarters.

After the last fell, Chaz said, "I've got a feeling Shai Khe isn't going to be surprised we're hot after him."

The general said, "No doubt. But, then, the surprise is at the other end, isn't it?"

At that point they entered the street of Shai Khe's headquarters. And at that moment all hell broke loose inside the warehouse.

They charged the door by which Shai Khe had entered their trap.

XXXII

Rider felt the smuggling craft nudge gently against a wharf. Sounds and odors told him they had docked along Tannery Row on Henchelside. The airshipmen, though tired, quickly made fast and left the ship. Moments later Rider heard the creak of oarlocks.

He popped out of hiding, surprised. And that was a mistake, for a guard had been left aboard. He was turning, drawing breath for a shout. Rider snagged the broken corpse of a single reeve stay block and hurled it. It thunked off the airshipman's forehead. The man went over backward.

Rider crept forth. He peered over the gunwale. Wonder of wonders. The spot of action had gone unnoticed, though the oarsmen in the two boats faced the ship.

Rider slithered to the wharf side and, when he was sure he would not be noticed, left the ship.

A group of urchins audience to everything gave him a hand—then scattered when he scowled.

He loped into the stench of Tannery Row, headed for King's Bridge, which lay a mile away. Thirty minutes later he was in hiding on the east bank, watching the airshipmen unload their prisoners and make their boats ready for a quick getaway. They left one guard again.

When the main party was out of sight he moved in. In moments he had the sentry trussed up and the boats adrift. He resumed his shadowing of the airshipmen. He caught up as they entered a warehouse.

He reached into the web and extended his senses, searching for signs of Shai Khe. There were none. But someone was there. And that someone was not friendly toward the easterner's men. A fight broke out. It was over in seconds, a successful ambush. Rider did not go investigate.

He suspected it would be wiser, tactically, to remain on the outside of events, unseen and unknown.

A wagon rolled up to the door Rider watched. Men from the warehouse loaded it with bound airshipmen, covered them with a tarp. Away the wagon went. A brisk, efficient piece of work.

The tough look of those men gave them away. They were air marines in mufti.

So. The next step was obvious. Wait for Shai Khe to come meet his people in a headquarters he believed to be secure.

There had been some busyness while he was off to Shroud's Head, that was certain. Despite his absence, his associates seemed to have Shai Khe on the run. But Rider had no great confidence in that appearance.

How long before the eastern devil showed himself? Not long at all.

It started like the row with the airshipmen. But that lasted only fifteen seconds. Then a brilliant flash illuminated the backs of the warehouse's few windows. The tenor of the uproar changed.

Rider was watching through the web.

Shai Khe had used a powerful spell to neutralize and incapacitate the marines, but before he could finish them off, Chaz, Su-Cha, and their gang broke in. The easterner had some bad moments with them. In fact, Chaz and General Procopio got in blows that nearly incapacitated Shai Khe.

Su-Cha used the sorcerer's moments of distraction and disorientation to shove Caracené into hiding and take her place.

Rider nudged the web and added to the confusion by undoing the spells binding the marines. Those gentlemen jumped up with blood in their eyes.

Shai Khe was not whipped yet. Not by a mile and a year. But he was rattled. The unexpected recuperation of the marines decided him to retreat and regroup.

He grabbed Su-Cha/Caracené's hand and took off.

Rider tugged the web just enough to make sure everyone in the warehouse was free and conscious. Then he withdrew and waited.

Shai Khe burst out the warehouse door. Fifty yards down the street he halted, whirled, hurled a vicious spell that undermined the warehouse's foundations. That whole nearer face of the building came down. Shai Khe headed for the river at a brisk walk.

The collapse should have killed all of the easterner's enemies. But Rider aborted that.

He had reached through the web and jammed an interior door. Chaz, the general, the marines, and the others had gone galloping toward the far exit before the collapse began.

Rider jogged to a parallel street, then raced to the river. He was sure Shai Khe meant to rendezvous with the airshipmen's boats. Shai Khe did things meticulously, calculatedly. He would know where the boats and ships made landings, for those points would have been preselected for his convenience.

Rider was in hiding not twenty yards away from the man he had left bound when the easterner loped into view, casting angry glances behind him. His enemies were closing in again.

He cursed once, softly, when he reached the river's edge and found his man unconscious and his boats gone.

He let go Caracené's hand, used both of his in a complicated series of gestures. The airshipman's bonds fell away. But he would not arise from his dreams.

Shai Khe faced his pursuers.

He seemed to swell in stature, in presence. An aura of great dread grew around him. The bowl of his uplifted left hand began to glow turquoise.

Chaz and the crowd were just thirty yards away. In almost ridiculous unison they stopped, flung themselves around, and scattered.

Shai Khe arced the blue fire after them. It floated through the air, trailing turquoise mists, crackling, leaving a rent in the web that was almost painful to Rider. The easterner either thought Rider out of the game or no longer worried about attracting his attention.

The blue fireball hit the street with an impact that rattled buildings for half a mile. It shattered. Pieces flew about, landing with their own thunderous impacts, fragmented, impacted, fragmented. Some chunks knocked holes in nearby walls. The smaller the chunk, the faster it moved and more dangerous it was. But the smaller pieces turned into mist more quickly, so remained dangerous for only a few seconds.

While the blue show ran, Shai Khe gathered his fallen henchman under one arm and Caracené under the other. With effortless ease. He raced toward the river, each step a longer one than the last. He did not stop because water lay in his way.

Water flew as if from huge hammerblows each time one of his feet hit. Rider was reminded of a skipping stone flying in reverse. Shai Khe's last bound to Henchelside was fifty yards long.

The easterner headed for the smuggler. And that pushed Rider into a tight moral bind.

The man he had left unconscious could ruin everything. He had but to tell his story. If Shai Khe was not totally suspicious already, finding his bridges burned before him.

Rider considered alternatives and discarded them. Each was self-defeating, requiring the expenditure of so much sorcerous energy that Shai Khe would be alerted anyway. The choices were two. Let Shai Khe be warned. Or work a small magic and close a man's mouth forever.

There was no choice, really. Shai Khe was a shadow intent on poisoning millions of lives. He could not be allowed to escape just to avoid taking the life of his minion.

Necessity made the thing no more pleasant.

Rider reached through the web and, as Shai Khe bounded aboard the smuggler, snapped a blood vessel in the airshipman's brain, behind the bruise left by the thrown block.

XXXIII

Shai Khe's feet hit the deck of the ship. He cursed, dropped his burden. A glance told him his man was dead. He whirled, began arcing a fireworks show toward the east bank.

Su-Cha decided it was time he absented himself from the sorcerer's company. To go on meant ever-increasing danger. And it was unlikely that Shai Khe would ever be less attentive than he was at the moment.

His intent was to slip over the side behind Shai Khe, hit the water, become a porpoise, and swim as if sharks were after him.

Rider saw Su-Cha begin to move, guessed his approximate intent.

He would never make it. A sorcerer of Shai Khe's attainments never became so angry or so distracted he failed to notice the movement of people around him.

Rider cooked up a little golden firework of his own.

This quite needless bombardment, which threatened to demolish the district, hinted that the easterner was fishing for a reaction anyway.

Su-Cha was not expendable. Neither were the people of the district.

Rider stepped out and delivered his apple-sized golden ball in one smooth motion. It streaked across the river. Halfway over it looked as if it would miss the smuggler by fifteen feet. Three quarters of the way over it began to slide to the right. In the last fifty feet it jumped.

It impacted upon the ship. Light flared. Timbers flew. A third of the smuggler burst into flames.

Mocking laughter and a volley of blue fireworks were Shai Khe's responses. He had won the roll, drawing Rider out.

Rider noted that Su-Cha was in the water.

He plucked another golden ball out of his left hand and hurled it. This one streaked straight toward Shai Khe. Another followed an instant later. Then another. The first died a hundred yards from the blazing ship, the second fifty. The third almost reached the easterner.

Shai Khe grabbed his surviving airshipman and bounded away, in leaps as long as those he had taken when he crossed the river. He trailed wicked laughter.

Rider's golden balls pursued him, through every twist and turn of his flight through Henchelside.

"Wondered when you were going to turn up," Chaz said, coming to stand beside Rider and glare at the burning ship.

"You played too long a bet," Rider admonished gently. "You'd all have been dead if I hadn't."

"I know." The barbarian was not the least chagrined as he added, "We didn't expect you. Glad you showed, though."

Others began leaving cover. Even a few residents began looking out to see if the storm had passed.

General Procopio lumbered up. "Good show! Eh? What? Got the beggar on the run. What next?"

"First we dig the woman out of the warehouse," Rider said.

Chaz gaped. "But… The sorcerer. He carried her off with him."

Rider chuckled. "That was Su-Cha again. He ought to be turning up any second, hungry enough to eat one of us." He was talking to the barbarian's back.

"And after Chaz saves Caracené? What then?" Greystone asked. The scholar looked exhausted, physically and emotionally.

"Then we loaf down to our yards and take a short airship ride." He peered across the river. Shai Khe was no longer visible, but his progress could be traced by the fireworks he tossed off as he went.

"He's going to turn into a ghost again in about two minutes."

"Maybe. But this time I know where he will do his haunting."

XXXIV

"Caracené!" Chaz bellowed. The interior of the ware-house was a ruin. Spears of sunlight stabbed down through dust almost too thick to permit breathing. He stepped past an eastern airshipman groaning beneath rubble which buried his legs.

"Caracené!"

"Here." The woman's voice was feeble, like the mewl of an injured kitten.

She was all right. Just shaken and dirty, looking as if she had been dragged twice around the chariot course at the coliseum. Chaz's concern weakened the moment he saw her safe. Then he recalled that she had started out a witch in apparent alliance with Kralj Odehnal, and only later had she melted into the sort of woman to whom he was more accustomed.

Shai Khe was clever and savage. She might be the sorcerer's ultimate piece to be played. Chaz felt he was not as clever as Rider or Greystone. He was more likely to stumble into something unpleasant. So he was a little cool, a little distant, as he helped Caracené to her feet.

She was not so cool. She threw her arms around his neck and clung tightly, shivering like a captive rabbit.

Rider chose a larger ship this time, one intended to survive the rigors of battle. Greystone argued for speed.

"Speed will not count in this," Rider said. "Survivability will. We're coming up to the face-to-face, where Shai Khe cannot duck us anymore. If it doesn't go our way, we want to be in good shape for getting out alive."

"You really think…"

"In an hour we'll see. He'll have to surrender or fight." Rider looked directly at Caracené. "Will he fight, knowing you are with us?"

Outside, one of the ground crew shouted that the airship lines were ready to cast off.

Caracené's gaze became evasive.

Rider repeated the question.

"He would fight," she admitted. "He cannot back down. Not for anything. He is totally committed."

Rider nodded. He surveyed his companions. "This is what we've worked toward… I have to warn you. It could go sour. This is as great a wickedness as has ever arisen. Does anyone want out?"

"Silly question," Chaz grumbled. "What I want is to get my hands around his throat."

Everyone else nodded.

"Take your stations, then. Tell them to cast off."

It was a bright, clear day. The Bridge was a broad blue highway running to the horizon. Its face was dotted with fishing boats and merchantmen. Rider viewed that traffic with concern. Someone down there could get caught in the middle.

"Shroud's Head," Preacher announced. He was steering the monster airship while Rider prepared for what was to come. "Battle stations, everybody."

Chaz sat Caracené in a seat usually reserved for an airship's commander. "You stay put till I tell you otherwise. You hear?"

Her eyes flashed fire, Rider noted. She had begun to show sparks of life. But she did as she was told, if only because it was the wisest thing she could do.

Spud joined Preacher in handling the airship. Chaz

and the others manned some of its weapons—though little good they might do in a confrontation between sorcerers the caliber of Rider and Shai Khe. Rider said, "Take station a half mile off the point, Preacher. Hold fast there. And wait." He seemed to go completely inside himself then.

Preacher and Spud did exactly as instructed.

Shroud's Head glared malevolently.

Nothing happened for a long time.

"What the hell?" Soup squawked suddenly. He pointed a shaky finger.

The air before Caracené had begun to glitter. The glitter became more intense, gave way to crawling patches of color that collided, mixed, spread, shone rainbow like oil on water. They formed the outline of a man.

"Our opponent wants to talk," Rider said.

As he spoke, the colors around the figure's head sorted themselves out and became fixed in the oriental features of the sorcerer Shai Khe. For half a minute those evil green eyes stared vacantly. They sparked then, recognized Caracené, shifted their gaze to Rider.

A hissing whisper seemed to come from everywhere at once. "So. Face to face now, Ride-Master. You have been a stubborn, resourceful, and lucky opponent, if foolish now. You grow overconfident, leaving the shield of your father's web. Go back. You are overmatched here."

"I was never overmatched. You have fled me time and again. But now there is nowhere you can run. Surrender yourself."

Soft, malicious laughter filled the cabin. "I was about to suggest you do the same. For the sake of the woman. You are a gentleman, Ride-Master, and would not see her destroyed. She is of value to me. I will give you and your men your liberty, after *you* have been disarmed, if you return her to me."

Rider did not respond. He stepped to a window, examined the Bridge. The broad blue strait remained sun-drenched and busy. Finally, he faced the image of the easterner. "Your hour is done. Give it up. Or suffer the consequences you bring upon yourself."

Rider's men stirred nervously.

"Brave, Ride-Master. But I am far too old to be bluffed that easily. Not even your father could do that." There was a glint of malice in Shai Khe's eye each time he mentioned Jehrke.

"As you will, then," Rider said. "I have warned you enough. Still, one last warning. Do not bring that airship out of Shroud's Eye. I disclaim responsibility for what will happen if you do."

Pure evil animated the sorcerer's laughter. Then he vanished.

A half hour had passed. Nothing had happened. Rider was growing concerned. Had Shai Khe, in his caution, readied one more bolt hole than expected?

"Think he's decided to take your advice?" Chaz asked.

"No. Though he may try to wait us out."

"He won't get anywhere doing that." Chaz pointed.

Four giants of the air were crossing the Bridge, two to either hand. Rider said, "Procopio. I believe we'll hear from Shai Khe soon enough now."

General Procopio had left the group back in the City. It had been his idea to land troops upon Shroud's Head, to prevent flight to the landward side. He had convinced someone very high up—maybe King Belledon himself.

The airships discharged their weapons as they passed the headland. The great stone face became spotted with fires. Several missiles penetrated the eye where Shai Khe's airship lay. The airships moved on. Soldiers slid down ropes.

A spear of emerald fire ripped out of the Devil's Eye. Its target was Rider's airship. Rider was ready. At a gesture the light bent heavenward.

Both of the monument's eyes began to burn an evil carnelian. Darkness gamboled behind the light.

The troops were all off the airships. They were linking up. Soon they would draw their line tighter.

The sea itself leapt at Rider's command, a foot-thick serpent of water rising to hammer the monument with its head. The power of that stream tore huge chunks from the stone face.

A horrible scream came from Shroud's Head. It grew louder rapidly. Just when it seemed it would become unbearable, it died.

The world was totally silent. And in the silence Rider's water monster collapsed.

The fires still burned in the monument's eyes.

The snout of an airship protruded from one.

"He's coming out," Preacher announced.

Rider nodded. "Back off. Don't let him get too close. Everybody hang on."

The pirate airship exited the Devil's Eye slowly—till its rear steering vanes cleared. Then it charged like a bull in the arena.

Rider sighed, both relieved and concerned. Such confidence might mean Shai Khe had no glimmer of his earlier visit—or it might mean that the easterner had detected it and taken steps.

Rider's airship backed down more slowly than Shai Khe's charged. The gap between ships dwindled. Chaz and the others readied their weapons. Without a battle complement Rider's ship would have a feeble sting, but still one stronger than the pirate's. The easterner would have no crew to spare for fighting.

A thin, almost invisible string of darkness connected Shai Khe's airship with the eye where Rider had detected the terror. The farther the easterner came out, the fatter and darker that line grew. Rider watched, face grim. "The man is smart and strong, but a fool at times."

The others did not understand. But Rider's face told them he had done something of which he was mildly ashamed.

A storm of sorceries exploded from Shai Khe's airship. Preacher dodged while Rider fended. Chaz discharged his weapon. Its flaring bolt arced toward the pirate, but fell far short.

The air before Caracené sparkled. Shai Khe's face appeared. A whisper of a voice said, "Now you meet the true despair, Ride-Master." The face vanished.

Rider looked sad.

The air itself shuddered as if from godlike hammer strokes. The black cable connecting the sorcerer's airship with the promontory fattened till it was as thick as a big man's waist. Then the landward end broke loose.

A globule of a darkness like nonexistence whipped toward Shai Khe's vessel. The eye could not fix upon it.

It impacted upon the easterner's airship.

The pirate folded like a sausage bent over a knee. "Move back now!" Rider ordered. "Move fast!"

Preacher needed no encouragement.

Everyone, on both ships, knew what would happen. But it was a long time coming—as though mocking by delay.

Shai Khe's ship folded almost double before a skin crack appeared where the strain of folding was greatest.

A gas bladder burst.

And that was the pirate's doom.

The gas exploded on contacting the air. Billows of fire flung out of the airship. The fire penetrated another bladder, which exploded in turn. The airship settled toward the water. New fires continued erupting.

Waves of heat beat against Rider's airship.

Rider took control and pressed closer, following the easterner down. Below, the nearest surface ships scurried away.

Two flaming crewmen jumped from the pirate. Rider tried to reach for them, to buoy them up, but without the web could not respond fast enough.

Gobbets of flaming ship dropped away, splashed into the Bridge, set the sea aflame.

"Holy Zephod," Preacher finally gasped. "I never saw one blow before. What a sight."

They all watched in awe.

"What's that?" Chaz asked, as the dying monster of the air started the final hundred feet of its fall.

"Sounds like…" Su-Cha frowned. "Sounds like somebody laughing."

The sound grew swiftly louder. And it *was* mad laughter.

Caracené made a startled, squeaky noise. Chaz whirled. He gasped. "Rider! You won't believe…"

Rider turned. A vast, sparkling face was taking form between him and the woman. Flames enveloped and distorted it. It was laughing.

It glared at Rider. Its laughter became mocking. All-enveloping words filled the cabin. "You have won nothing, Ride-Master. Nothing. Even I am but a messenger." More laughter, rising toward the insane.

The phantom snapped out of existence.

The pirate airship hit the water. A last half-dozen gas bladders erupted at once. A violent updraft staggered Rider's airship, sent it rising and whirling. He fought for control, finally got the vessel moving toward Shasesserre.

"What did he mean, he was only a messenger?" Chaz demanded. His question was for Rider but he was looking at Caracené.

"I'm not sure," Rider replied.

"Well, I don't like it."

"I'm not sure I do, either. In some ways this has been almost too easy a victory."

"Too easy?" Su-Cha squawked.

Chaz glared at Caracené. "Woman?"

But Caracené remained silent. She stood at a window now, staring back at the nest of fire and flock of smoke celebrating Shai Khe's destruction.

XXXV

Neither Rider nor his men bragged up what had happened. But countless others had been in the affair. They talked. In fact, most of the City had become aware of the struggle before its conclusion. So when it became generally known that the threat from a great devil of a sorcerer out of the east had been overcome by Jehrke's son, there developed a general acclamation of the son as Protector in his father's stead.

King Belledon was not pleased.

Repercussions continued for some time, as the King purged or exiled the last of those who had conspired against Shasesserre.

Border situations that had threatened all along the empire's frontiers evaporated almost magically. The troublesome easternmost provinces fell into an abnormally peaceful state. Agents in those far lands said the report of Shai Khe's demise had paralyzed the eastern sorcerer's shadowed kingdom of terror. The great peril was at an end. The thing was done. Even King Belledon sent Rider his grudging gratitude and congratulations.

But the world was filled with illusions, and the greatest illusion of all was that of safety.

Not for the first time, Preacher asked, "What did Shai Khe mean when he said he was only a messenger?"

Rider had not forgotten that. He, Greystone, Spud, and Su-Cha all were scouring their sources and resources in an effort to prepare for possible troubles.

They unearthed no news of any value—not even a concrete indication that Shai Khe had been anything less than his own agent. They found only the faintest wisp of a rumor from the nethermost east about a cabal of which Shai Khe might have been a junior member. But that was only hearsay of a rumor of hearsay.

Chaz figured that in Caracené they had the next best thing to a primary source. "Press her," he told Rider, in private. "She knows a lot that she isn't telling."

Rider raised an eyebrow. It was an expressive querying gesture. Chaz reddened slightly. He had been paying elaborate public court to Caracené. And she seemed pleased by his attention.

"Not yet," Rider replied. "We're not under the sword. She has been a slave—and more. She needs time to rediscover the meaning and bounds of her freedom. She has to determine for herself if she has a moral obligation to speak or to remain silent. With Shai Khe gone, and with his hold upon her charred and sunken beneath the Bridge, I can see no reason to doubt that she will come around. It will have far more meaning when it comes from the heart. Exercise your famous barbarian patience. Take her out on the town. Take her to the Little Circus. General Procopio is giving three days of games to celebrate his part in our success."

There had been some grumpiness over Procopio's having claimed so much. Rider, though, was pleased because the old officer was diverting attention from himself and his men.

"Take her out and buy her a western-style wardrobe. I do not know women well, but never heard of one whose morale could not be improved by a shopping spree. Especially when someone else is picking up the cost."

Chaz grumped, "I think she looks just fine wearing what she has."

"You would. Most of the time she's half-naked. But she can't wander the streets like that."

Chaz grumped some more, mostly because he had fixed notions of the way women shopped. He did not look forward to squiring Caracené around the courtiers of the City. But he went out and collected her.

He knew his duty. And there was a fine chance that doing it would earn him pleasant rewards.

XXXVI

General Procopio invited Rider's gang to share his personal box at the Little Circus—reluctantly, after Chaz accused him of ingratitude and glory-hogging. Since the public were well aware that the Protector's son—himself acclaimed Protector now—was primarily responsible for thwarting the danger to the City, a few bitter words could make of the Procopio Games the disaster of the social season. The general issued his invitation rather than risk humiliation.

Other than Chaz, only Greystone evinced much interest in attending. The scholar had worked out systems for betting on horse and chariot races and wanted to test them in the field. Su-Cha would have attended had he been allowed, but the law was adamant about forbidding his kind to attend sporting events, the outcome of which might be mystically jiggered. Too many bettors' money might be affected.

Caracené was both elegant and exotic in a white pleated creation which fell to her ankles but left her arms bare. Her hair was in a single twist that came around her neck to the right and fell between her breasts. Chaz felt drab and inadequate as they made for Procopio's private box. Ten thousand eyes measured Caracené and found her beauty more than adequate. A thousand men murmured their admiration and asked one another who that beauty might be.

Chaz felt smaller than ever.

But he was carrying his sword, his illegal sword, without challenge, so those who mattered did not lose track of his identity amidst Caracené's radiance. That was reassuring.

The box of honor was shaded by a gaudy awning. The only other seating so honored was the royal box. Chaz dropped onto one of the stone benches. "Thanks for small favors." He pointed upward. "It's days like this that make me wonder why I never stayed home." It was hot, yes, and very humid.

General Procopio turned, held a finger to his lips. Charioteers were getting themselves aligned for a start and the herald was about to announce the contestants.

"You haven't told me anything about your homeland," Caracené whispered.

"Neither have you, Sweetheart. Sounds to me like we're even."

Greystone had arrived before Chaz and Caracené. He was seated behind the general, calculating on a wax tablet. He turned and scowled.

"Do they have chariot races there?"

Chaz eyed the woman suspiciously. Why this empty-headed act? "No. Pony races. Bareback. Through the woods."

Procopio and Greystone both scowled. The herald had begun announcing the charioteers and the stables they represented. Caracené got the message, if Chaz did not. She folded her hands in her lap and watched the race get under way.

Chaz hardly noticed. A shadow too small for that of a cloud or airship, yet big, was rippling over the crowd. Some people were looking up instead of following the race. He stepped to the edge of the canopy, caught a glimpse of a large wing vanishing beyond the stadium rim. "Su-Cha clowning around?" he wondered.

"I don't think so." Greystone startled Chaz, who had not seen the scholar rise. "The runt has more style. The bird is big but dingy. He'd be colorful."

Rising crowd noise kept Chaz from responding.

The chariots were running hub to hub going into the back stretch. The mob expected real excitement going into the final turn.

"It been here before?" Chaz shouted.

"All morning. Here it comes again."

"Looks like a giant chicken hawk," Chaz opined. "My size."

Caracené moved up beside him. When she saw the bird she gasped and lost color. Chaz asked, "You know what that thing is?"

Caracené nodded. As she opened her mouth to say something, Procopio shouted, "If you people can't keep it down back there, go away."

The bird turned a half circle, one yellow eye fixed upon the stadium somewhere above Procopio's box.

Caracené gasped again, and lost more color.

The bird folded its wings, falling into an attack dive. Its plunge was directly toward Chaz.

He hurled Caracené and a squealing Greystone into the concealment provided by the awning, dragged his blade out and braced himself.

The chariots were into the final leg of the race, the three frontrunners still neck and neck. The crowd was shrieking. Only a few spectators, quite close, noted Chaz's actions and looked up. They out-shrieked the race aficionados.

As Chaz prepared to meet his death Caracené bounded to her feet and rejoined him. Her hair was aflame. Her eyes had become whirling pools of smoke. She flung her hands toward the hawk. They glowed like red-hot steel.

The bird staggered just yards from completing its strike. That saved Chaz.

It smashed into the awning, shrieking and snapping at him over its shoulder. Beneath the canvas people scrambled. The bird ripped fabric and flesh with its talons.

Chaz swung his blade in a flat arc, scored the monster's beak and opened flesh nearby. His backstroke pruned feathers from a wingtip. The beast seemed of mixed minds. It wanted to face and fight him while continuing to rip at those still trapped beneath the canopy.

It dipped its head, snapped its beak, came up with a severed human arm. Chaz bounced a sword-stroke off its forehead, peeling flesh back. Blood flooded its eyes. It shrieked and dropped its booty, flung itself up to attack with its talons. Chaz clipped more feathers from the same wing, batted one monster foot aside with his blade, rolled beneath the other. From flat on his back he drove the tip of his sword into the beast's belly. Though he caused only a minor wound, the bird screeched and tried to flee.

It flung itself into the air, wings thundering. But with blood-blinded eyes and one wing trimmed it could not fly a straight line. It plunged into the crowd fifty yards away. People screamed as it began killing anyone it could reach.

Chaz gained his feet, ripped the canvas off the remains of those who had occupied Procopio's box, dreading what he might see when he found Greystone.

But the little scholar was fine. He had stretched out against a stone bench where it was impossible for the bird to reach him.

Procopio had been less fortunate. It was he who had lost the limb.

Chaz roared and looked for the bird.

It had tried to fly again, and again it had plunged into the crowd. The panic was spreading. In a rage, he prepared to storm through the mob on a quest for revenge.

Caracené's touch stayed him. He looked down into her eyes. They had returned to normal. Her hair no longer blazed. Her face was drained. Once she had his attention, she pointed.

He looked up a dozen rows. He saw a tall, grey-haired gentleman in antiquated apparel who stood calmly observing the growing terror. As his gaze swept over Chaz a taunting smile tugged at his lips.

"Green eyes!" Those awful green eyes! "It's him!" Chaz roared. "It has to be him." He hurled himself out of Procopio's box.

The old man strode away. The chaos parted for him as though he were fiery to the touch.

Chaz did not have the same luck.

A hammercrack of sorcery rang out over the stadium. Every hair on Chaz's head stood up and crackled. The monster bird screamed once, died.

In the moment he was looking away Chaz lost track of the grey-haired gentleman with the green eyes. He cursed.

Then he sighted Rider and Su-Cha ploughing through the crowd, headed his way.

XXXVII

"What brought you here?" Chaz demanded when Rider reached him.

"Caracené twisting the web. What happened?"

"She tried to stop that bird. I don't know where it came from, but I know how it got here. Shai Khe brought it."

"But…" Su-Cha piped.

"I saw him. Caracené pointed him out. Where is she? He had greyed his hair and was wearing old-time clothes, like one of the Cynics, but it was him. Not his brother or cousin or uncle or whatever you're going to say, but him. There aren't any other eyes like his eyes. Where's Caracené gotten to?"

"There is no strain on the web," Rider said, scanning the crowd. "Su-Cha, start looking for him."

Chaz was looking around now, quietly desperate, seeking Caracené. He did not catch a glimpse of her. He had remained calm throughout the crisis. Now he was ready to panic.

"Keep a watch for the woman, too," Rider told Su-Cha. He started down toward Procopio's box.

"Can't you feel her?" Chaz demanded.

"She isn't leaving any trail in the web."

"It's *his* fault. Shai Khe. He did something to her. She was almost ready to come over to our side. How could he have survived an airship's destruction? Especially with that shadow of his trying to gobble every soul in sight?"

"I don't know," Rider confessed. "I'm as mystified as you. I was convinced that he was dead. But he is old and powerful and tricky."

"I'm going looking, too. He isn't getting away with Caracené if I've got anything to say about it."

"I don't know how he could have gotten through that alive," Rider repeated. "Unless he was not aboard the airship at all. Which could have been, though I don't see how he could have managed the airship so deftly from ashore."

Chaz, a glob of moroseness feeling sorry for itself huddling in a corner, did not look up. No slightest trace of Caracené or the green-eyed man had come to light yet.

"We'll hear from Shai Khe again," Rider said. "If, indeed, it was he that Chaz saw." Rider was not convinced that his only witness was reliable. "His ego wouldn't let it be otherwise." What was meant to be a feather of hope fell flat with Chaz.

"If it was Shai Khe, I'm convinced he has left the City. He would have to do so. He would need to restore the edifice of terror that began crumbling with the report of his death. If he lives, and Caracené is with him, he will be in the east and we will have report of them soon enough."

But the big northerner refused to be encouraged.

172 ~ GLEN COOK

"I'll find her," he mumbled. "I'll find them both. And when the dust settles there won't be no more green-eyed spook doctor hanging around. No more slave-master for her to be afraid of."

Rider looked at his friend with compassion, but he said nothing more. There was nothing to say. What was needed now was the passing of time.

It would be a time shorter than any of them imagined.